Suno Kahani Meri
Listen To My Story

Suno Kahani Meri (Listen to my story)

FATHIMA HIMANA

Published by FATHIMA HIMANA, 2025.

First edition
Published by: Fathima Himana, 2025

This book is a work of fiction. Names, characters, places, and incidents are either products of the author's imagination or are used fictitiously. Any resemblance to actual persons, living or dead is purely coincidental.
Typeset in Bembo by Fathima Himana
Digital edition prepared in [Kandy, Sri Lanka]

This is a work of fiction. Similarities to real people, places, or events are entirely coincidental.

SUNO KAHANI MERI (LISTEN TO MY STORY)

First edition. October 9, 2025.

ISBN: 979-8232926649

Written by FATHIMA HIMANA.

To those who learned too late, and to those who still have time. May Hina's story be a gentle reminder that every moment of kindness is a precious gift and that love should never wait.

About the Author

Fathima Himana was born in Kandy, Sri Lanka. From a young age, she loved writing short scripts and stories, often scribbling down thoughts to make sense of the world around her. While on bed rest following hospitalization, she felt life moving around her while she remained still. In those quiet moments, she began to write, turning her observations and emotions into a story **'Suno Kahani Meri'** that is not her own but carries moments and feelings she has witnessed in the world around her. Beyond writing, she loves spending time with her mother, from whom she learns invaluable lessons about life, strength, and compassion. For her, writing from the heart is the best way to connect with readers. Suno Kahani Meri is more than a story it is a reminder that even in pain and uncertainty, love and hope endure.

Acknowledgements

This novel was written entirely on my own, but I would like to thank the people who supported me along the way. To my mother, for always encouraging me and believing in my dreams, even when I doubted myself. To my best friend, for listening, inspiring, and cheering me on every step of this journey. And to anyone who picks up this book and reads my story, thank you for sharing in the emotions and moments that live within these pages. Your time, attention, and openness mean more than words can express. Every story comes alive because of those who believe, listen, and feel alongside it, and for that, I am truly grateful.

Chapter 1

'There are stories written in silence,
Felt only by those who live them.'

Ayzen, a 28-year-old man standing six feet tall, with broad shoulders and a strong, well-built body, stood at the balcony of his family's grand house in Chakwal. His thick, dark beard framed a sharp jawline, and his black eyes were so intense they seemed to notice everything around him. His hair was thick and dark, kept neat but natural, giving him an effortless charm. His face had high cheekbones and a straight nose, with full lips that sometimes curved into a quiet, confident smile. He moved and stood with the kind of calm confidence that made people notice him without him even trying. Girls often whispered about him, drawn not just to his looks but to the quiet strength he carried. His deep, steady voice, the way he looked at someone without rushing, and the natural grace in his movements made him someone people remembered.

From the balcony, he could see the village below, winding streets, small homes glowing with warm yellow lights, and children running and laughing along the dusty paths. The breeze rustled the mango trees in the courtyard, carrying the fresh, earthy smell of the farms nearby. He breathed it in slowly, feeling the calm evening around him.

To anyone looking, it seemed like a perfect life with wealth, family, and power. But inside him, there was a hollow space, a wound that refused to heal.

Five years ago, Ayzen's life was simple. He worked hard, laughed easily, and never thought too much about the future. Then came a wedding. It was his friend's sister's wedding, and honestly, Ayzen hadn't expected much from it. Just another village wedding with bright lights, loud music, and endless cups of chai. He went more out of obligation than excitement. But as he entered the courtyard, with the sounds of drums and laughter around him, he noticed someone who made him stop for a moment. She had just walked in with a group of cousins, not overdressed but still impossible to miss. Her peach coloured dress flowed down, her dupatta pinned neatly but slipping just enough to seem intentional. She was fair skinned, the warm lights of the courtyard making her skin look almost golden. Her face was round but with sharp, defined features that gave her a striking look-not the soft, doll-like beauty some girls had, but something bolder. Her brown eyes scanned the courtyard slowly, as if weighing everything and everyone. Her lips, naturally pink, were pressed into a slight curve that could almost pass for a smile. Her hair was tied loosely at the back, a few strands falling across her face in a way that almost looked careless but never messy, as though even that was deliberate. She looked around twenty-one, young but with a confidence that made her seem older, as if she already knew how to hold herself so people would notice her. She didn't rush or fidget like the other girls; she moved slowly, as if she owned the space around her. There was confidence, yes, but also a hint of pride that made her seem distant. Her smile was small, almost secretive, as though she was amused by everyone else.

Then, a child ran up and tugged at her dress. She bent down to help, her bangles jingling softly. It wasn't a warm, playful gesture, it was careful, and precise, like she was making sure people saw her being "kind". Ayzen didn't know why he kept staring. Something about her felt like a puzzle.

Graceful yet a little cold, approachable but not quite warm. She was unforgettable; Ayzen's heart started beating faster. He didn't even realise when his legs moved; he rushed toward his friend, barely able to take his eyes off her.

"Yaar, who is that girl?" He whispered urgently, pointing at her from across the courtyard.

The moment his finger lifted, Mahnoor's eyes suddenly turned toward him. Their gazes met. A cold shiver ran down Ayzen's spine. For a second, it felt like time froze. His mouth went dry, and he quickly lowered his hand, but it was too late; she had seen him. His heart hammered in his chest, not knowing if she would get offended, make a scene, or simply look away. His friend leaned in and said casually,

"Oh, that's Mahnoor. She's a distant relative of mine."

Before Ayzen could recover from the shock, Mahnoor started walking toward them. Each step felt slower than the last, almost like it was happening in slow motion. Ayzen's palms grew sweaty.

What if she slaps me in front of everyone? He thought.

She stopped right in front of him, her brown eyes steady on his.

"Hey," she said, her tone calm, not harsh, and surprisingly friendly. "I saw you pointing at me. Can I know the reason?"

Ayzen blinked, caught off guard. He quickly shook his head and said,

"I'm sorry... I just wanted to know who you are, that's all."

She tilted her head slightly, her lips curving into the faintest of smirks.

"Why? Do you think I'm cute?"

For a second, Ayzen was stunned. How does she have the courage to ask that? He thought his mind racing. No girl had ever spoken to him like that before. Before the silence could stretch too long and turn awkward, Ayzen's friend stepped in with a grin.

"Mahnoor, this is Ayzen, my friend. Ayzen, this is Mahnoor."

The tension eased as they exchanged a quick, polite smile. What followed were a few minutes of casual, harmless chat, mostly small talk about the wedding, the food, and the music. But for Ayzen, those few minutes felt like the most important conversation he'd had in years. Even after she walked away to join her cousins, Ayzen couldn't take his eyes off her.

His heart was still pounding, and his mind kept replaying the moment the way her brown eyes had held his, the slight tilt of her head when she asked him that bold question. Every detail seemed sharper, brighter, and alive. He found a quiet corner in the courtyard, pretending to sip his chai, but all he could think about was her. The laughter around him, the music, the clinking of glasses none of it mattered. All that mattered was Mahnoor and the way she had made him feel nervous, excited, curious, and a little unsteady all at once. He remembered how her smile had been small, almost secretive, and how it didn't quite soften her sharp features.

Yet, that made her even more intriguing. There was something in her-a spark, a confidence, and a quiet pride that drew him in and made him want to know her story, her thoughts, even the smallest details of her life.

Every time he caught her looking back at him, a shiver ran down his spine. Her presence seemed to linger around him, even when she was out of sight. Ayzen felt a strange mixture of fear and longing. Fear because he didn't know her, didn't know if she was kind or cruel, playful or dangerous. Even as the wedding celebrations carried on around him, Ayzen kept stealing glances at her. Every small movement-the way she laughed with her cousins, the way she adjusted her dupatta, the way she paused to speak to an elder made his heart beat faster. It was like watching a puzzle he desperately wanted to solve, but part of him was afraid that the pieces might not fit the way he hoped. And deep inside, he knew one thing with startling clarity: this girl, Mahnoor, had just walked into his life, and she was not going anywhere. Not from that night, not from his thoughts, not from the hollow space inside him that had long waited for something or someone like her.

As he was lost in thought, still replaying every moment of seeing Mahnoor, a gentle voice pulled him back to reality.

"Ayzen, what world are you in, beta?"

His mother asked, placing a hand lightly on his shoulder.

He blinked and turned toward her, suddenly aware of how far away he had drifted in his own mind. Slowly, he pointed toward Mahnoor, who was now talking with her cousins a little distance away.

"Ammi," he said softly, almost unsure, "look at her."

His mother followed his gaze, her eyes landing on Mahnoor. For a moment, she smiled warmly, as if she could see the same spark that had captivated her son.

"She looks beautiful, Ayzen," she said, her voice full of gentle approval.

"Such a graceful girl. I like her already."

Ayzen felt a small warmth in his chest at his mother's words. For the first time that night, he felt a little less nervous and a little more daring. Somehow, knowing that his mother saw what he saw that Mahnoor was special made everything feel a little more real, a little more possible. Mahnoor had felt a thrill that night, a quiet happiness that she rarely let herself show. Someone had noticed her, really noticed her, and that someone was Ayzen, a handsome young man. The thought made her smile to herself as she found a way to slowly get his number, careful to seem casual, as if it had all been by chance.

The next day, as Ayzen sat at his desk, buried in notes and preparing for an important exam, his phone buzzed. A new message popped up. He picked it up, and his heart skipped a beat. It was Mahnoor.

"Hi... It's Mahnoor," the message read simply.

Ayzen's fingers trembled slightly as he typed back, trying not to sound too eager. What started as casual texts, talking about the wedding, the village, his exams, and her studies, soon grew into long conversations. They shared small jokes, late night thoughts, and little pieces of their lives. Each day, Ayzen's heart grew a little fuller, and each day, Mahnoor's smile and her clever words kept him hooked.

A year passed like this, their love growing stronger in messages, calls, and stolen moments together. Ayzen dreamed of the day he could formally bring a proposal to Mahnoor's house. But when that moment finally came, she gently but firmly pushed him away.

"Not yet... There's time," she said, her words soft but decisive.

He was hurt, but he understood. Determined, he decided to move to Dubai for a year to focus on work, thinking the distance might make their eventual reunion sweeter. But while he was away, the calls became fewer. The messages slowed. She told him she was busy with studies. Her words were polite but distant. He tried to call her one evening after returning, excited to speak to her, but she cut the call before he could say more. His heart sank, confusion and worry gnawing at him. Unable to bear the silence, he decided to visit Mahnoor's house. He wanted to understand the situation, to see things clearly.

When he reached the gate, what he saw shattered him. Ayzen's hand tightened around the gate, his heart already pounding, and his chest heavy. And then he saw them. Mahnoor stepped out of a sleek car, her small bag swinging lightly from her shoulder. A young man, unfamiliar to Ayzen, gently took her hand and pulled her close. She didn't resist; instead, she leaned into him as he hugged her. The kind of hug that spoke of familiarity, of love, of a bond Ayzen had once imagined only he could share with her. The warmth in their closeness, the quiet laugh she gave him, the way her eyes softened for him-every detail was a knife twisting in Ayzen's chest. Ayzen's knees buckled. The air seemed to thicken around him. His chest tightened until it felt impossible to breathe.

Every step he had taken toward her, every message, every dream of a life together, felt like a lie he had told himself. A year of hope, waiting, and loving all crumbled in a single moment. The man helped Mahnoor with her bag and whispered something that made her smile. Then he kissed her gently on the forehead, a gesture reserved for someone who belonged to him. The realisation hit Ayzen like a thunderbolt: this man wasn't just someone in her life. He was her husband. When the man turned back toward his car, his eyes caught Ayzen standing frozen by the gate. He frowned, stepping closer, his voice sharp with suspicion and authority.

"Who are you?" He demanded, looking Ayzen up and down. "Why are you here?"

Ayzen could barely speak. His voice trembled, cracking under the weight of shock and despair.

"Who... who are you to Mahnoor?" he whispered, as if asking the question aloud might make it untrue.

The man's expression hardened. "I'm her husband," he said, his tone calm but final, leaving no room for argument. Then, his eyes narrowed, and he asked again, suspicion and challenge in his voice, "And who are you?"

Ayzen's chest felt like it had been crushed. His throat was dry. He could barely catch his breath. Words failed him, but the look on Mahnoor's face-the softness, the warmth, the smile meant for someone else shattered him completely. Everything he had believed in, everything he had waited for, all the late-night conversations and shared dreams, felt like ashes slipping through his fingers. His hands shook. His knees felt like jelly. The cold of the evening seeped into his bones, but it was nothing compared to the freezing emptiness that spread through his heart. He wanted to scream, to beg, to ask why, to know a reason or anything to make the world right again. But no words came. He could only stand there, a broken shell, watching the life he had imagined with her already exist with someone else. Tears blurred his vision, but he didn't care. The pain was deeper than anything he had ever felt, a weight that pressed on his chest and threatened to crush him. Every memory of her, the smile that had made his heart race, and the soft laugh he had imagined sharing with her now cut him like glass. But he couldn't let Mahnoor's husband see the truth; he couldn't ruin their life together, not like this. Taking a deep, shaky breath, he forced his voice to stay calm.

"I... I'm just an old friend of hers," he said, his words barely above a whisper.

The man's eyes narrowed, suspicious. He calls Mahnoor outside.

"He says he is your friend. Is that true?"

Mahnoor's eyes widened when she saw Ayzen standing there. For a brief moment, fear and panic flashed across her face.

"Y-yes... he is an old friend of mine," she said quickly, her voice almost trembling.

The husband, satisfied, left, giving them space.

For a moment, there was silence. The Mahnoor who had once smiled at him with warmth, who had laughed with him, now stood there like a stranger-sharp, angry, and untouchable. Her gaze cut through him.

"You... you need to leave. Now," she said, her tone laced with anger and finality.

"Never show your face here again."

Ayzen felt tears sting his eyes, but he couldn't stop. "Mahnoor... please... tell me why. Why couldn't you wait for me? Were you forced into this marriage? Did they..."

She cut him off with a bitter laugh, sharp as a knife.

"No. He is better than you. He earns more, and he keeps me happy. It's your fault you weren't enough. I have dreams too, Ayzen. I need a man who can give me everything I want, everything I deserve. Were you capable of that?"

Ayzen's heart felt like it had been shattered into a thousand pieces.

"But... I was building myself... for us, for our future. I was working hard. I was..."

Before he could finish, Mahnoor stepped forward, pushing him towards the gate. Her hands were firm, her eyes cold. "Enough. Leave. Never come back." The gate slammed shut behind him before he could even utter another word. Ayzen pressed his hands against it, his tears falling freely now. His chest ached so much it felt like it might burst. The girl who had once spoken to him so sweetly, and laughed with him so lightly had transformed in an instant and been replaced by someone he no longer recognised. He sank to the ground outside the gate, broken, hollow, and unable to understand how the world had turned so cruel.

Every hope he had nurtured, every dream of their life together, had been ripped away. And all that was left was emptiness so deep it threatened to swallow him whole.

'Brokenness is not the end;
It is only the beginning of a story.'

Ayzen returned home that evening, exhausted, hollow, and broken. His steps were heavy, each one seeming to echo the weight pressing on his chest. The house, normally familiar and comforting, felt unbearably quiet, almost mocking in its stillness. His mother saw him as soon as he walked in. She froze for a moment, alarmed by the expression on his face: pale, eyes red-rimmed, shoulders slumped.

"What happened, beta?" she asked softly, moving toward him.

Ayzen could barely speak. The tears he had tried so desperately to hold back now spilt freely. He sank into his mother's arms, clutching her as if she could shield him from the world. "She... she left me, Ammi... she... she's gone... and it hurts so much..." His voice cracked, broken by grief and disbelief.

His mother held him tighter, feeling the depth of his pain. Her own tears welled up, blurring her vision. "Ayzen... my son... I'm so sorry. You are a good, kind man.

You deserve someone who sees your worth, someone who loves you for you. Don't let this break you completely. You will find happiness again, a better girl, a better life. I promise you that."

Days passed slowly. The world continued moving around him, but for Ayzen, time felt suspended. Every street he walked, every corner of his home, and every sound reminded him of what he had lost. He realised, with a painful clarity, that dwelling on the past was stealing his health, his energy, and his peace.

One day, he made a decision-quiet, firm, unshakeable. He would never let himself be weak to another woman's whims again. He would not let love make him weak. His heart was bruised, but his mind was clear: he would focus on himself, on building a life that could never be taken from him. He poured himself into work. Every hour, every project, every sleepless night became a step toward reclaiming his dignity and his future. He studied business, learnt new skills, met people, and gradually, brick by brick, slowly, he built his own company, '**NovaTech.**'

Years passed. The boy, who once was full of hope and naive love, had transformed into a man of his own making. A self-made CEO respected and admired. A man who lived on his own terms, who answered to no one but himself, and who had learnt to find fulfilment in his achievements. Yet, even in his success, the memory of Mahnoor lingered as a shadow of the past, a reminder of the pain that had once threatened to break him. But now, it was tempered with strength, a quiet resilience. He had turned heartbreak into ambition, and loss into purpose. He was no longer defined by the love he had lost but by the life he had built a life full of control, independence, and self-respect. And though the wound of Mahnoor's betrayal would never fully disappear, he carried it as a reminder of what he had endured and how far he had come. He had built walls around his heart, refusing to trust love again.

Love, he had decided, was a dangerous game he would never play.

Chapter 2

Ayzen's family lived together in a big, lively house that was never quiet for long. His father, strong and wise, often tried to get him to relax and enjoy life "Beta, take a break for once," his father would say with a small smile, ruffling his hair, but Ayzen just nodded and smiled. His mother, gentle and caring, moved around the house quietly, making sure everyone had eaten and everything was in order. She worried about him but never pushed too hard, knowing some things a mother couldn't fix. The house was always full of energy, but it was more than just a home; it was a place of respect. People from the village and neighbouring towns often came by, seeking advice, help with disputes, or guidance in business matters. They greeted Ayzen's father and uncles with respect, bowing slightly or shaking hands, speaking softly, as if the walls of the house themselves carried authority. The family's opinions carried weight, and their name was well known for both influence and generosity.

In the house His siblings brought constant noise and life. Zara, twenty, was cheerful and always talking, preparing for her medical college classes. Then there were the twins, Aleeza and Zaroon, both twenty-three. Aleeza quietly working from home, focused on her tasks, and Zaroon teasing his brother and sister, always joking and laughing. Hamza, twenty-five, Is helping Ayzen with his business, learning the family ways of managing people and respect. Ayzen's extended family also lived in the house, his father's three sisters and two brothers, along with all their children. Cousins ran through the corridors, voices echoing with laughter, playful shouting, and teasing.

There was always someone cooking, someone calling for someone else, someone telling stories, or someone making a joke. The house was never empty, always warm with love, chatter, and the noise of a family that lived together in every sense. Through all this, Ayzen moved like a calm shadow present, noticing everything, yet distant. He saw his siblings joking, his cousins laughing, and his mother arranging tea, but he remained apart, quiet and composed, like someone who belonged but also kept a space just for himself.

Meanwhile, in another corner of Chakwal, a cheerful voice rang from a small house. "Ammi, did you see my socks?" Hina called, tugging at her bag as she spoke. At twenty years old and standing five feet tall, Hina was small but full of life. Her long black hair fell straight down her back, a few strands brushing her round, dark brown eyes that sparkled with curiosity and mischief. Long lashes framed her eyes, giving her gaze a soft, innocent charm. Her lips were naturally pink, and her tan skin glowed with youth and health. She wasn't too slim, not too heavy, just perfectly balanced, with a presence that made people notice her without effort. Hina always wore a shawl, draped carefully over her shoulders, a quiet sign of her modesty. But the shawl couldn't hide her playful nature. She laughed easily, moved quickly with energy, and carried herself with a calm, gentle confidence that made everyone around her feel at ease.

Life hadn't always been easy for her. She had lost her father when she was just five and had grown up with her mother, learning resilience and independence along the way. But Hina never let hardships dim her spirit. She studied hard, worked hard, and dreamed even harder.

And deep inside, she always imagined a life with a man who would love her more than anything, someone whose care would make her feel safe, cherished, and understood.

That morning, as Hina adjusted her bag and readied herself for college, there was a quiet excitement in her heart. The sun peeked through her small window, painting the room with golden light, and the faint smell of fresh breakfast drifting from the kitchen made her smile. Her best friend, Zara, was already waiting outside, her bright energy impossible to miss. "Come on, Hina! Don't keep me waiting," Zara called. Hina laughed softly and straightened her shawl, feeling a rush of warmth at her friend's enthusiasm. Together, they stepped out onto the busy street, the morning air carrying the scent of fresh bread from a nearby bakery and the distant hum of village life. They walked quickly, chatting and giggling, the sounds of their laughter blending with the clatter of rickshaws and the chatter of people heading to work. They chatted casually, laughing about small things; the new teacher, a funny incident from yesterday, and the upcoming assignments. As they settled into their classroom, Zara leaned closer and whispered with excitement,

"Hina, did you hear? There's a big party at college in two days! Everyone's talking about it."

Hina's eyes lit up.

'Really?' I didn't know. What are you going to wear?"

Zara giggled, twirling a strand of her hair. "I'm not sure yet. I think I'll wear something bright, something fun. What about you?"

Hina smiled softly, imagining herself at the party.

"I... I don't know. I'll see. Maybe something simple. I just want to enjoy it."

That afternoon, Hina walked home slowly, her thoughts still on the upcoming college party. She imagined the decorations, the music, and the laughter and, most importantly, what she could wear. Her steps slowed as she reached her small house, the familiar creak of the door greeting her. Inside, her mother was busy in the kitchen, the aroma of simmering food filling the air. Hina hesitated for a moment, biting her lip.

"Ammi... there's a big party at college in two days," she said softly, trying to sound casual. "I... I need a dress for it."

Her mother looked up, worry and caution in her eyes.

"Hina... We don't have money for fancy clothes. You should focus on your studies. Don't think about going to a party," she said gently but firmly.

Hina felt a small pang in her chest. She nodded quietly, forcing a faint smile.

"Yes, Ammi," she said softly, her voice barely above a whisper. Once she reached her room, the door clicked shut behind her, and the sadness she had tried to hide poured out. Tears pricked her eyes as she hugged herself tightly, feeling both disappointment and longing. After a while, determination replaced the sadness. She remembered an old wedding dress of her mother's, tucked away carefully in a corner of the cupboard. It was a soft purple colour, delicate and slightly shimmering, a fabric that looked rich and elegant even after all these years. Hina carefully took it out, running her fingers over the texture. Her heart raced as she imagined herself wearing it at the party, laughing, dancing, and blending modesty with elegance. Hina worked quietly for hours, adjusting, cutting, and stitching the dress to her size. By the time she finished, she held it against herself in front of the mirror. Her long black hair fell freely down her back, her round brown eyes shone softly, and her naturally pink lips curved into a small smile. She had no makeup, not even a touch of it, yet she looked like a princess. She twirled gently, imagining the lights, the music, the faces of her friends, and the feeling of being noticed, not for her wealth or appearance, but for her presence, her confidence, and her grace.

That night, Hina could barely sleep. She lay on her bed, staring at the ceiling, her mind spinning with excitement and imagination. She thought about the dress, the party, the laughter, and how she would move and smile, pretending she wasn't nervous. Her heart beat a little faster with every thought, the anticipation almost making her restless. She imagined every little detail: the glittering lights, her friends' reactions, and the feeling of stepping out into a world that, for just a few hours, belonged entirely to her.

Even though she had no makeup, no fancy shoes, and no one to guide her, Hina felt like she had created magic all on her own. A quiet smile spread across her face as she hugged her pillow. This party, she thought, might just be the moment her dreams began to shimmer a little closer to reality.

The college party day arrived; it was already in full swing. Lights hung from the ceiling in bright colours, music thumping softly in the background. The air was warm and lively, carrying the mixed scents of perfume, food, and flowers. Students moved in groups, laughing and dancing, sharing stories and snacks. Hina felt herself drawn into the energy around her, letting the rhythm of the night lift her spirits.

She danced a little, laughed a lot, and for the first time in a while, felt completely free. Hours passed quickly. Music, chatter, and laughter filled every corner, and Hina lost track of time. By the end of the night, as the music slowed and people started saying their goodbyes, she realised she hadn't thought about how she would get home. Her bag was still slung over her shoulder, and the streets outside looked unfamiliar in the dim, flickering light of the streetlamps. A small knot of worry formed in her chest. Just then, Zara's phone rang. She answered quickly and then turned to Hina with a relieved smile.

"Hina, my brother is on his way. He'll drop you home too."

Hina nodded, a flutter of nerves mixed with excitement stirring inside her. She had heard about Zara's elder brother, Ayzen. But had never met him. She only imagined him from the stories Zara had told: tall, handsome, strong, and a little... distant. It was almost eleven at night. The college gates were quiet, lit softly by the yellow glow of the streetlights. Hina and Zara waited, bags in hand, chatting softly to pass the time. Hina's heart beat a little faster; she had heard stories about Zara's brother, but seeing him in person was a thought that made her stomach flutter. Then, from the distance, a sleek black car glided toward them. Its polished surface shone under the streetlights, reflecting the glow like a moving jewel. There was something almost royal about the way it moved-smooth, quiet, commanding attention without noise. The car stopped in front of them. The door opened, and Ayzen stepped out. He was tall, impossibly tall, six feet of strength and presence. Broad shoulders, a straight posture, every movement measured and calm. His dark hair was perfectly in place, catching the soft light, and his sharp jawline gave him an air of quiet authority.

His deep, dark eyes seemed to look through the night itself, serious yet somehow alive with something unspoken. Hina felt her breath catch, her heart skipping a beat. He walked toward Zara with effortless confidence, but even in that simple movement, there was a grace, a power that seemed to pull everything into his orbit.

The night breeze swept past, lifting a few strands of Hina's hair, and in that moment, she felt as though the world had slowed down. Every step he took, every subtle motion, made him seem larger than life.

"Come on, let's go home," he said to Zara, his voice calm, deep, and steady, carrying a quiet authority that left no room for argument.

Zara's face lit up. "This is my friend, Hina. Can we drop her home too?"

Ayzen didn't even glance at Hina. "Okay," he said simply, his voice low but firm, yet there was an edge of something distant in it that made Hina's chest tighten. She climbed into the backseat, her shawl wrapped tightly around her shoulders, unable to stop her gaze. Even as the door clicked shut and the engine purred to life, she felt as if the air in the car had shifted heavy and alive. He drove with absolute control, hands firm on the wheel, every movement precise, and his eyes scanning the dark road ahead. Hina tried to focus on the passing streetlights or the faint hum of the engine, but it was impossible. Her eyes kept drifting to him, taking in the straight line of his shoulders, the sharp angles of his face, and the way his jaw tightened slightly as he concentrated. There was something untouchable about him, something that made her feel small and aware at the same time. Strong, silent, and magnetic even in silence.

Hina's heart raced. She had never seen anyone like him before, and though he hadn't even looked at her, she felt as though her world had quietly shifted the moment he stepped out of that car. Hina felt a strange warmth spreading through her chest, a mix of curiosity, admiration, and something she couldn't yet name. She noticed the way his fingers gripped the wheel steady, and confidently, each movement calm yet deliberate. The subtle flex of his muscles as he adjusted the car slightly made her pulse quicken. Even his silence spoke volumes. There was a quiet force in him, a presence that made the air around him feel different, alive. Every small detail-the way his dark hair caught the dim glow of the streetlights, the shadow of his jawline, the faint crease in his brow-seemed to etch itself into her mind. Hina tried to focus on the world outside, the quiet streets passing by, and the occasional rustle of the trees, but it was impossible. Ayzen dominated her attention without even trying.

She wondered what he thought, what stories were hidden behind those deep, serious eyes. It felt as if he carried a whole world within him, one she could sense but not reach, and yet that distance drew her in even more. The quiet hum of the engine, the soft glow of the streetlights, and the occasional chirp of a night bird everything-seemed to fade except for him. Hina's heart raced, her mind spinning, but she forced herself to sit still, careful not to stare too obviously. Every now and then, he spoke to Zara, but even then, the calm authority in his tone was undeniable. There was no arrogance; only control, precision, and an unspoken command that made the space around him feel charged. Hina felt drawn to him all at once. As the car neared her street, her thoughts were a whirl of fascination and nervous excitement. She adjusted her shawl again, trying to compose herself, but it was useless. When the car finally slowed and stopped, Hina felt a pang of disappointment. The ride was over, but the impression he had left was just beginning to take hold. She stepped out carefully, her eyes lingering on him for a fraction longer than she should have. Even then, he didn't look at her, but somehow, just by existing, he had shifted the pace of her world.

Suddenly a gust of wind blew down the quiet street, and Hina's shawl slipped from her shoulders, tumbling into the middle of the road. She froze, her heart skipping a beat. Without hesitation, Ayzen stepped out of the car. He walked confident steps, picked up the shawl, and gently wrapped it around her. Every movement was quiet and strong, yet he didn't give anything away. Hina looked at him, and her eyes were drawn to his face. He didn't glance at her, not once. But to her, it felt like his whole presence filled the space. His broad shoulders, sharp jawline, and quiet strength made her chest tighten. And then, she saw his eyes dark, serious, and unreadable. He wasn't looking at her, but she felt as if his gaze was the only thing she could see. Her heart raced. Warmth spread through her chest, a flutter that made her breath catch. He said only one thing, softly, "Take care," and walked back to the car. No smile, no glance, nothing. And yet, she felt like he had left a mark on her, a spark she couldn't ignore.

Hina stepped into her house, still wrapped in her shawl, her mind racing. She barely noticed the dim light in the hallway or the smell of dinner that had gone cold. Her thoughts were only on him. His calm, silent presence, the way he had handled her shawl, the untouchable intensity in his eyes. She could replay that moment over and over and still feel her chest flutter.

"Where have you been, Hina? It's almost midnight! You can't come home this late!"

Her mother scolded from the kitchen, voice sharp but tired. Hina only nodded absentmindedly, her mind elsewhere. She didn't even hear the words properly. Hina goes into her room and closes the door softly behind her. She didn't even notice her mother's faint scolding fading away in the hallway. Her mind was still on him. She slowly walked to the mirror, her shawl still draped around her shoulders. For a moment, she just stared at her reflection, her dark brown eyes wide, cheeks slightly flushed, and lips pressed together. Then, almost without realising it, she began to speak softly, pretending he was there.

"Why do you have to be so... untouchable?" she whispered, tilting her head, a shy smile on her lips. "Why do you make me feel like this?" She traced her fingers along the edge of the mirror, as if reaching out to touch him, imagining his hands strong and steady, giving her warmth. "Do you even know what you did to me?" she murmured, her voice barely audible. Hina laughed quietly at herself, a mix of embarrassment and delight. She was talking to a man she barely knew, yet in her heart, it felt like he had been there with her the whole night. Her eyes lingered on her reflection, and she imagined his calm, dark gaze looking back at her, intense and unreadable. For a long while, she stayed like that, lost in her own little world, pretending he was standing in front of her. Every movement, every word she whispered, felt alive, real, and somehow thrilling. Finally, she let out a soft sigh, a mixture of longing and excitement. She knew she would remember this night forever, the first time she had felt drawn to someone so completely, so unexpectedly.

• • • •

THE NEXT DAY AT COLLEGE, Hina found Zara waiting outside thc classroom.

"Good morning, Hina! How was your night?" Zara asked, grinning.

Hina smiled shyly. "It was... fine. Just a little tiring, I guess."

Zara laughed. "I know, right? That college thing went on forever. Did you enjoy yourself?"

"Yes... it was nice," Hina replied, her thoughts drifting back to last night. She bit her lip, feeling a little flutter in her chest.

Zara leaned closer, teasing. "You were quiet yesterday. Not your usual chatter. Something happen?"

Hina hesitated and then shook her head. "No... nothing." She smiled softly, trying to hide the way her mind kept replaying the black car and the tall, serious man who had picked them up.

Zara smirked knowingly, nudging her. "Come on, Hina. Don't act all innocent. Was it my brother?"

Hina blinked, cheeks heating. "Uh... maybe," she murmured, looking away quickly.

Zara laughed, her eyes twinkling. "I knew it! You're thinking about him, aren't you?"

Hina swallowed, trying to stay calm. "I was just... noticing things," she said softly, her mind replaying every detail; his height, his eyes, the quiet way he moved.

Zara teased further, shaking her head. "Well, you're not alone. He doesn't really let anyone close, though. No girlfriends, ever." Hina nodded, feeling a mix of excitement and curiosity. Even Zara's teasing couldn't stop her thoughts from returning to him, to the mysterious, untouchable man who had left such a strong impression. All day at college, Hina couldn't focus. She tried to listen to lectures, take notes, and follow the discussions, but her mind kept drifting back to him. The image of Ayzen stepping out of that sleek black car, his quiet authority, and the way he had wrapped her shawl around her shoulders kept replaying in her mind. Zara noticed her friend's distraction almost immediately. "Hina, are you even listening?" she whispered, nudging her lightly during class.

"I... I am," Hina mumbled, cheeks flushing, trying to hide the daydream that had completely taken over her mind. But Zara wasn't convinced. She grinned mischievously. "Hmm... sure you are. Dreaming about my brother again, right?" Hina gave her a small, embarrassed smile, looking away. "Shh... don't say that," she whispered, but inside, her heart was racing just thinking about him. Even during lectures, Hina's eyes wandered to the window or to the ceiling, imagining him standing there, tall, broad-shouldered, and untouchable. She replayed every small detail; the way he moved, the strength in his presence, and the deep, dark eyes that hadn't even looked at her yet made her heart flutter uncontrollably.

Her daydreaming didn't go unnoticed. Midway through class, the teacher's sharp voice broke her trance.

"Hina, could you please stop daydreaming and come to the front of the class?"

Hina's heart sank. She stood quickly, her cheeks burning as she walked to the front. The whole class snickered quietly, and Zara gave her a teasing wink. Hina felt embarrassed but couldn't help smiling faintly to herself, remembering that fleeting moment with him. By lunch, Zara continued teasing. "Careful, Hina. If you keep staring off like that, you'll start imagining him handing you a crown or something," she joked.

Hina laughed softly, hiding her face behind her hand. "Zara! Stop it," she whispered, but secretly, she loved thinking about him just a little more. Even as they walked back to class, Hina's mind couldn't leave him. Every movement, every thought seemed to return to that tall, silent man, whose presence had quietly stolen her attention, leaving her daydreaming.

Two days later,

Hina was packing the bag in college, ready to go home, when Zara called her and said.

"Wait, Hina! I have to take something to my brother. Mom packed his lunch," she said, a teasing sparkle in her eyes.

Hina hesitated. "You... you mean Ayzen?"

Zara grinned. "Yes! Don't act like you didn't want to see him again."

Hina's cheeks flushed, but she followed Zara, curiosity and excitement swirling inside her.

The office building gleamed under the afternoon sun. As they entered, Hina's eyes widened. Through the glass walls of the meeting room, she saw Ayzen seated at the head of the table, completely focused. His broad shoulders filled the chair, crisp shirt perfectly pressed, dark hair in place, and that sharp jawline she couldn't forget. Hina noticed a young woman, probably a colleague, trying to get his attention. She smiled, leaned forward slightly, and laughed at something he said, hoping to catch his gaze. But Ayzen didn't look at her. Not once. His eyes stayed on the papers in front of him, his movements precise and calm. He acknowledged her only with a slight nod.

Hina's chest tightened. She couldn't take her eyes off him. There he was, six feet of quiet authority, ignoring flattery and attention as if it didn't matter. It made him even more admirable. Every gesture-his hands adjusting the pen, the way he leaned in to read a document, the subtle furrow of concentration on his brow made her heart race. Zara set the lunch on his desk.

"Here, Bhai, Ammi made your favourite," she said cheerfully.

Ayzen looked up briefly, his piercing eyes meeting Zara's. "Thank you," he said, his voice calm, deep, and measured. He didn't glance at Hina, but she felt the power of his presence wash over her. Hina couldn't help stealing glances, captivated by the way he carried himself. Strong, disciplined, manly, yet untouched by vanity or attention. The young woman's flirting had no effect on him; he remained utterly in control, and it made him irresistible in Hina's eyes. As Zara winked at her, Hina stayed frozen for a moment, imagining what it would be like if he noticed her, if he spoke to her. Her heart pounded, and strange warmth filled her chest. Even without a single word directed at her, he had left a mark she couldn't ignore.

As they walked away from the office, Hina couldn't hide her frustration.

"Zara! Why did you bring me there? I... I could barely breathe!" she exclaimed, tugging at her bag strap nervously.

Zara laughed, a teasing glint in her eyes.

"Oh please, Hina. Don't try to act all innocent. I know you liked it!"

Hina's cheeks flushed bright red.

"Liked it? Are you crazy? I...no, I didn't!" She stammered, trying to sound firm but failing miserably.

Zara nudged her playfully.

"Hahaha, come on! Your little daydreaming face gave you away. Admit it you couldn't stop staring at my brother."

Hina scowled, hiding her face behind her hand, but she couldn't stop a small smile from forming.

"You're impossible, Zara," she muttered.

"I know," Zara said with a smirk.

"And that's why I'm your best friend. But trust me, Hina... you're completely smitten. Don't try to hide it from me or yourself." Hina sighed.

The walk home was quiet, the streets almost empty, and Hina's mind kept replaying the afternoon at Ayzen's office. By the time she reached her house, the fatigue of the day weighed on her, but her thoughts refused to settle. She quietly entered her room, leaving her shoes by the door, and slipped under the covers. The faint glow of the streetlight outside filtered through the window, casting soft shadows across the room. Hina lay there, eyes wide open, thinking about Ayzen, his tall, commanding presence, the way he had ignored attention and the calmness in everything he did.

Chapter 3

It was a Saturday noon, and Hina found herself sitting at home, bored and restless. Her books lay open on the table, but her mind wandered aimlessly. Suddenly, an idea struck her, making her heart beat a little faster. She rushed to her mother, tugging at her sleeve.

"Ammi, I have assignments to do... Can I go to Zara's house? We're in a group, so it's important to do it together," she said, trying to sound convincing.

Her mother looked surprised.

"Zara's house? You never go there. Why now? You usually do your assignments on your own."

Hina bit her lip, nodding quickly.

"No, Ammi... This one is difficult. I really need her help too."

Her mother studied her for a moment and finally said, "Okay, if you need help, then go." Hina's face lit up instantly. She jumped in excitement, her heart racing. She hurried to get ready, picking out her dress carefully, adjusting her shawl just right, and making sure she looked presentable. Once ready, she grabbed her bag and stepped out, her steps quick and eager, excitement bubbling inside her as she headed toward Zara's house for the first time.

For the first time, Hina stepped into Zara's house. The moment the huge gate opened, she felt as if she had entered a palace. The driveway was wide and lined with flowers, the walls painted a creamy white, and the sun glinted off polished marble floors. Servants moved quietly in the background, carrying trays and tidying things, adding to the sense of order and grandeur. Hina couldn't help but pause and take it all in, her eyes wide as she admired the tall ceilings, the sparkling chandeliers, and the intricate wooden carvings on the doors. Every corner seemed to whisper wealth, a world so different from her own. As she hesitated, a lady came rushing toward her, her expression a mix of curiosity and suspicion.

"Who are you?" she asked sharply.

"I-I'm Zara's friend," Hina stammered, adjusting her shawl nervously.

The lady's eyes flickered over her from head to toe.

"Stay here. I'll call Zara," she said briskly before turning and leaving, her heels clicking loudly on the floor.

Not long after, the lady, Zara's aunt, ran from room to room, excitedly announcing in her dramatic voice,

"Everyone, Zara's friend is here!"

Her words carried judgement, exaggerated for effect, as she hurried to gather family members.

Within minutes, the entire household were there before Hina, murmuring among themselves, their eyes curious and sharp as they looked at Hina. Hina's chest tightened, her fingers clenching the strap of her bag. She had never felt so scrutinised, so out of place in her life. Just then, Zara appeared, her bright smile immediately putting Hina at ease.

"Hina! Welcome, come sit," she said warmly, taking Hina's hand and guiding her to the plush sofa in the living room. For the first time, Hina felt a small spark of comfort. Her heart was pounding not from fear but from excitement and maybe a little nervous anticipation. No one else seemed to welcome her, but Zara's kindness made her feel slightly at home. Still, her heart secretly longed to see Ayzen. She stole glances around the house, hoping he would appear, imagining him walking past with that quiet authority that had left her breathless. Before she could fully settle, Hina's ears caught harsh whispers from the other side of the room. Zara's family were speaking in low but sharp tones:

"Zara, why are you spending time with her? Girls from her background only come for money and connections."

Hina froze, her chest tightening, a sting of sadness hitting her like a physical blow. She lowered her gaze, her mind flashing to her father. If he were still alive, maybe she would be seen differently; maybe she wouldn't have to face these harsh judgments. A single tear threatened to escape, but she pressed her lips together and took a deep breath, forcing herself to push aside the hurt. She had come here to study and maybe, just maybe, to catch a glimpse of Ayzen.

Hina's heart was racing. She had been waiting quietly, sitting on the edge of the sofa, her fingers nervously twisting the edge of her shawl. Every sound in the house seemed amplified. And then... she heard it.

"Ammiiiiii! Is lunch ready?"

The voice was deep, strong, and somehow commanding, yet casual. Hina's eyes darted toward the source. There he was, Ayzen. He stepped out of his room, tall and effortless in a simple brown t-shirt and black trousers. The sleeves hugged his toned arms perfectly, the veins along his forearms standing out as he stretched. Even from where she sat, Hina could see the subtle strength in his biceps, the way his shoulders moved with each step. He was breathtaking, and her stomach fluttered uncontrollably.

He stretched his arms, yawned slightly, and called out again.

"Ammiiiiii!" His voice echoed lightly through the hall.

Hina held her breath, hoping he would look her way, but he didn't. His sharp eyes scanned the corridor and finally caught a glimpse of Hina sitting nervously in the living room. For a brief moment, he registered her presence, but it didn't faze him. He didn't stop, didn't glance her way again, and simply carried on with his routine. He moved toward the kitchen, opening cupboards and fetching the lunch his mother had prepared; his every motion was admirable. The slight veins on his forearms flexed as he lifted the plates, the brown t-shirt hugging his strong frame. He hummed softly to himself, completely absorbed in his task, as if the world contained only him and his work. Meanwhile, Hina's heart raced uncontrollably. She felt a storm of emotions-excitement, nervousness, and longing-all swirling inside her.

Butterflies danced in her stomach, yet he remained oblivious, unaware of the fluttering girl in the corner of the room. Then Hina and Zara finished their assignments. Hina packed her books carefully, a bright smile spreading across her face. Today had been different; being at Zara's house, seeing Ayzen, even just for a little while, had filled her with a strange, happy energy she couldn't explain.

As she stepped out onto the street, the evening breeze brushing against her cheeks, she couldn't help herself. She twirled once, then twice, letting her joy spill out in little steps and soft spins. Her shawl fluttered lightly as she danced down the quiet lane, her heart feeling lighter than it had in a long time. She laughed softly to herself, imagining the look on Zara's face if she saw her like this. Every small movement, every step, felt like a secret celebration of her day, of the little moments that had made her heart flutter. For a brief while, the world seemed brighter, the air sweeter, and Hina felt, in those tiny, carefree steps, that happiness could exist even in the simplest of moments. By the time she reached home, her cheeks were flushed. She tiptoed inside, careful not to wake her mother, and couldn't stop thinking about the day, the assignments done, the glimpses of Ayzen, and the strange, thrilling feeling that followed her like a shadow.

After that day, Hina found herself going to Zara's house more often, always with the excuse of working on assignments together. Each visit gave her a chance, even if small, to catch a glimpse of him. The thought of him made her heart flutter, and somehow, studying together with Zara became the perfect excuse to be near him. But it didn't take long for Zara's family to notice.

One afternoon, as Hina and Zara were busy with their books, Zara's mother frowned from the kitchen.

"Zara, why does your friend Hina come here so often? You barely go to her house!"

She called out.

Zara bit her lip, glancing at Hina, who felt her cheeks warm.

"Ammi, we're just working on college assignments. She needs my help, that's all."

Zara replied, trying to sound casual.

Her mother wasn't convinced.

"Assignments every day? This is too much. Be careful with the kind of people you let into our home,"

She warned.

Hina froze, overhearing every word. Her chest tightened, a mix of sadness and frustration bubbling inside. She felt the weight of her own background. Yet, she swallowed it all, forcing a small, polite smile. She wouldn't let it ruin her day. Assignments were done, and for her, this was the only way to sneak a moment of happiness, to be close, even from afar, to the man who had captured her attention completely.

That day at home, Hina's mother called out from the kitchen, her voice sharp but full of worry.

"Hina! Come here; you have to think about your future. You can't keep dreaming and forgetting the reality!"

Hina took a deep breath, standing firm.

"Ammi, I don't want to think about marriage now. I want to become a doctor. That's my dream, and I will make it happen."

She said, her voice steady, though her heart raced with determination. Her mother sighed, a mix of frustration and love. She knew her daughter had spirit, but the world was not easy for girls like them. She shook her head, returning to her chores, silently hoping Hina would understand the struggles she would face.

Meanwhile, far away, in the quiet mansion, Ayzen was absorbed in his work. His world was disciplined, controlled, and perfectly organised. He had no time for distractions. Yet, unknowingly, a single encounter from the other night, simple meetings with Hina, had begun to stir something in his carefully structured life. Neither Hina nor Ayzen realised it, but slowly, silently, destiny had started weaving their paths together.

Chapter 4

Hina arrived at Zara's house in the late afternoon, carrying her books and assignments. The garden was quiet and calm, the sun casting a warm glow over the neatly trimmed grass. She and Zara sat under the big neem tree, spreading out their notebooks and pens, chatting casually about college and their assignments.

"So, did you understand the last lecture?" Zara asked, flipping through her notes.

Hina nodded, but her mind wandered. She kept sneaking glances at Ayzen, who was leaning against the other side of the garden, phone in hand, talking to someone about business deals. He was completely absorbed, dark eyebrows furrowed in concentration. Even when he spoke, his deep voice was calm. Hina's heart skipped every time their eyes accidentally met. She quickly looked down at her notebook, cheeks heating up, pretending to focus on the equations and diagrams in front of her. Zara noticed her friend's distraction and smirked.

"What? You're not even paying attention. Daydreaming again?"

Hina bit her lip and shook her head, forcing a smile.

"No... just... thinking about the problem."

Zara laughed softly. "Uh-huh, sure. Thinking. You mean him, right?" she teased, nodding subtly towards her brother.

Hina's face turned bright red, and she whispered,

"Zara, don't say that!"

Meanwhile, Ayzen was completely unaware of the teasing between the girls. He was so focused on the calls and messages that he barely noticed them sitting nearby. After a while he noticed her gaze. For a split second, her eyes met his. Ayzen frowned slightly, puzzled.

Why on earth is this girl looking at me like that?

He wondered silently.

Does she have a crush or something?

He shook his head, annoyed with himself for even thinking about it.

Who cares...? He said.

Still, despite himself, a tiny smile appeared on his lips, barely noticeable, just enough to show he had seen her. It was quick, and faint, and said nothing, yet it felt like a validation. Then, as quietly as he had noticed her, he turned and left the garden, walking inside to focus on his work again. Hina's heart skipped a beat at that tiny smile. She couldn't believe it was just a small, quiet smile, yet it made her feel like he had noticed her in a way no one else ever had. She stayed there a little longer, trying to calm her racing heart, but her thoughts kept drifting back to him.

Zara nudged her.

"Focus, Hina... the assignment."

She whispered, smiling knowingly. Hina shook her head, trying to concentrate, but her mind was still tangled in thoughts of Ayzen, the man who barely noticed her yet had somehow left a mark on her heart.

So, every time she came to Zara's house, he would pass by without even looking at her. He didn't talk to women at all, as if that part of his life was locked away forever. People whispered that he had loved someone once, but something had gone wrong, and since then, he had built walls around his heart. Hina couldn't stop herself from loving him. His silence, his distance, only pulled her closer. She tried to ignore it, and tried to tell herself that someone like him would never choose someone like her. But the more she tried, the stronger her feelings grew. One evening, lying awake in bed, she started worrying.

What if one day he marries someone else? What if he never even knows how much I love him?

The thought made her chest hurt, so she decided she couldn't keep it bottled up any longer. With shaking hands, she sat down and wrote him a letter. She poured everything out-her love, her dreams, and her pain-as if she was speaking to him face to face. When she was done, she stared at the paper, her heart beating so hard she thought it might burst. For a second, she thought about tearing it up.

But she didn't.

She folded the paper carefully.

'He has to know', she told herself. Even if he rejected her. Even if it broke her heart. At least he would know. With that, the night passed.

The next morning, Hina woke up with her heart racing. She hadn't slept properly all night, thinking about the letter. She clutched it tightly as she got ready, her hands sweating. By the time she reached Ayzen's office, her legs felt like they might give up. The tall building and glass walls made her feel even smaller. People in formal clothes walked past her, busy with their lives. She walked up to the reception desk and asked softly,

"Can you... Can you please tell Ayzen Sahib that someone wants to meet him?"

The worker gave her a curious look but nodded and left. Hina sat there, her heart thumping so loudly she thought everyone could hear it.

After a few minutes, the worker came back.

"Sir is in a meeting. He can't come right now."

Her stomach dropped. For a second, she almost turned and ran away. But then she remembered why she came. She swallowed hard and said,

"Please tell him... I left something for him. It's under the brown book on his table."

Before she could change her mind, she walked quickly to his office, slipped the folded letter under the heavy brown book on his desk, and left. Her heart was beating so fast.

When Ayzen came back later, the worker casually told him,

"Sir, a girl came earlier. I don't know who she was, but she said she left something for you under the brown book on your desk."

Ayzen frowned slightly, surprised but too busy to think about it. He loosened his tie, sat down, and poured himself some water. His phone buzzed with messages, pulling him back into work. The letter just sat there, quiet and hidden, waiting for him to notice.

But destiny wasn't done yet...

Later that afternoon, the office door burst open without a knock.

"Ayzen bhai!"

Anoosha's cheerful voice rang out before she even stepped inside.

She was his phuppo's (aunt's) daughter, just twenty-two, pretty and stylish, and always dressed like she had stepped out of a fashion magazine. Her confidence filled every room she entered, and she knew it. Anoosha had always been the centre of attention in family gatherings, and she loved it.

But Ayzen barely looked up from his laptop.

"Anoosha,"

He said flatly, rubbing his temple.

"I'm busy. Don't touch anything on my desk."

She ignored him completely, strutting across the room in her heels and spinning into the chair opposite him.

"You work too much, bhai. You're going to look fifty before you even turn thirty."

She teased, twirling the pen that sat on his table.

He sighed, clearly annoyed.

"Anoosha, please. I have calls to make."

But Anoosha had the habit of poking around where she wasn't supposed to. As she leaned back, her eyes landed on the brown book on the table. Something white peeked out from underneath.

"What's this?" she said, her curiosity sharpened, reaching for it.

"Anoosha,"

Ayzen's tone turned sharp, his eyes narrowing.

"Don't disturb me."

But it was too late. She had already pulled the folded paper free. As she unfolded it, her teasing smile froze. Her eyes moved quickly over the words 'soft', 'heartfelt', 'almost trembling' on the page. A confession. A declaration of love. At the bottom, in neat, nervous handwriting: ***Hina.*** Anoosha's lips curved into a slow, knowing smile. Her arrogant, playful nature lit up with interest. This was not just any letter. This was drama, and Anoosha loved drama more than anything. She folded the paper carefully, almost too carefully, and slid it into her designer purse before Ayzen could stop her.

That night, the house was full of warmth and noise. The servants moved in and out, setting bowls of curry and stacks of steaming rotis. Everyone was gathered around the long dining table: Zara, her parents, her brothers, the whole family and Anoosha, who sat with her usual pride, twirling a spoon between her fingers. Ayzen was quiet, as always, scrolling through his phone with a serious face.

Barely touching his food. Then Anoosha leaned back dramatically, holding up the folded letter. Her mouth twisted into a smug smile.

"Should I tell you all something interesting?"

She said, her tone playful but sharp.

Ayzen immediately looked up, his dark eyes locking on her hand.

"Anoosha,"

His voice was calm but heavy with warning.

But she only smiled wider.

"No, everyone has to hear this."

She said, her excitement rising. And before anyone could stop her, she unfolded the paper and began to read. The first few words were soft, almost tender-a confession of love. The whole table fell silent. Even the clinking of spoons stopped. The air felt heavy. Zara's father leaned back in his chair, his face darkening with every word. Anoosha's voice grew dramatic, savouring every line.

"...I know you will never look at me, but still my heart only chooses you..."

The room went silent. Ayzen's phone slipped from his hand and hit the table with a dull thud. His face betrayed nothing, but inside, something shifted: confusion, shock, even anger.

Who could have written this? He thought.

Anoosha dragged the moment until the very last line and then spoke the name with satisfaction.

"Hina."

The name hit the room like thunder. Zara gasped softly, her fork clattering on the plate. Her father's face turned red with rage.

"That girl?"

His voice boomed, echoing through the hall.

"The daughter of that poor woman? How dare she write such a letter to my son?"

Ayzen didn't move. His jaw clenched, his fists tightening under the table. His mother shook her head, her voice bitter.

"I told you, Zara. These people only come close for money. See? She used friendship with you to trap her way into this house."

"No, Ammi!"

"Hina is not like that," Zara tried to defend her.

But her father slammed his palm on the table.

"Enough! From today, I don't want that girl near this house. Tell her to stay away!"

The entire table fell silent again, the air thick with anger. Ayzen's chair scraped back suddenly as he stood. His face was unreadable, neither agreeing nor defending, just cold. Without a word, he walked out of the dining room, his footsteps echoing in the hall. Upstairs in his room, he sat alone. The letter lay in his hand now. He read it again, slower this time. The words were soft but brave, every line heavy with feelings she must have kept hidden for so long. He leaned back in his chair, exhaling sharply.

'Why him? Why her? What was she thinking when she wrote this?'

For the first time, Ayzen wasn't just annoyed. He was unsettled. This was no ordinary confession; it was raw, and real, and it refused to leave his mind. Then His mind wandered back to the last time he had let someone close. The last time he had trusted someone with his heart and how they had broken it. That girl had left him, walking away without a backward glance, leaving him with nothing but a scar he carried quietly ever since. 'And now, this?' He said to himself. Another girl. Another confession. Another storm he hadn't asked for. His jaw clenched. He wasn't angry at Hina, not yet. But he was angry at fate, at life, at how it never left him alone. He closed his eyes briefly, steadying himself, before looking up again and having a deep breath.

Three days later, Hina walked into Zara's house, her heart light and ready for their usual study session. But the moment she stepped inside, the warmth she had expected was gone. The house felt heavy and silent; the servants avoided her gaze, whispering behind her back. Something in the air made her chest tighten, and for the first time, Hina felt a creeping fear she couldn't name. As she entered the living room, her worst fears came true. The entire family was there, staring at her like she was a stranger, their expressions sharp and unforgiving. Anoosha was the first to speak. With a cruel smirk, she tossed the folded letter at Hina's feet.

"So, this is the girl who thought she could reach our family with words," she said, her voice loud and mocking.

The words pierced Hina like knives. Hina bent down to pick up the letter, hands trembling, but before she could say anything, the shouting began. Voices of anger and disappointment filled the room.

"Do you know your place?" Zara's father barked.

"Do you even understand who you are trying to reach?"

Her grandmother joined in, her words sharp and biting. "Girls like you only think about money! How dare you even dream about our son?"

Hina's tears flowed freely now. She pressed her palms against her face, trying to stop the trembling in her lips, but it was impossible. Her chest ached, and the world felt unbearably heavy. She could feel every gaze as a blade cutting deeper and deeper.

She wanted to disappear, to vanish from that grand house that had suddenly become a cage of judgement and shame.

Then, Ayzen appeared at the gate. Hina's heart leapt; maybe he would stop this. Maybe he would protect her. But when he looked at her, his eyes were steady, serious, and unreadable. He didn't scold anyone; he didn't argue. Instead, he spoke directly to her, his voice calm, low, and firm.

"Hina... Forget this. Focus on your studies," he said.

Even though the words were gentle, there was no warmth of affection, just a clear, brotherly distance. But somehow, they carried a tiny comfort, a hint that he didn't want to humiliate her further. She stared at him, tears streaming, chest aching. His words didn't erase the pain, but they gave her the smallest sense of safety, like a hand brushing hers without touching. Ayzen turned and walked back inside, leaving Hina standing frozen. Hina ran from Zara's house, her legs moving almost on their own. Her chest felt heavy, and her hands shivered as if they had a life of their own. Each step echoed in her mind, carrying the weight of the words, the laughter, and the cruel glances. By the time she reached her own street, her breath was ragged, and tears had already started falling.

As soon as she stepped inside, she barely noticed her surroundings. She climbed the stairs two at a time, her heart pounding so loudly she feared someone might hear it. In her room, she closed the door and sank onto her bed, clutching her pillow tightly as though it could absorb the pain. Tears streamed down her face, soaking the pillow, her sobs muffled into it so her mother wouldn't hear. She cried and cried, her body shaking with heartbreak, each breath coming in short, painful bursts. The room was quiet except for her quiet cries, the world outside forgotten. She reached for her phone, desperate to call Zara, to hear her friend's voice, but Zara's parents had already taken her phone away. Panic and loneliness surged in her chest.

No one could reach her, and she could reach no one. Her heart felt utterly isolated, raw with pain, the night stretching endlessly around her.

That night, Hina lay in her bed, her body exhausted, her heart shattered. She pressed the folded letter to her chest, feeling its weight, feeling every unspoken word, every dream she had dared to imagine. Her tears soaked her pillow, her mind replaying every glance, every sharp word, and every cold, unblinking look from Ayzen. She had loved quietly, and deeply, and it had only brought her pain. For now, she would hide her love, swallow her tears, and let the world move on, even as her heart refused to forget him.

Chapter 5

Weeks passed like slow rain. Hina tried to bury herself in books, to memorise names, places, and theories and to prepare for upcoming exams. It was a clear Monday morning. The sun came soft through the window, and Hina's Ammi was at the stove, patting warm flatbreads. The house smelt of fresh dough and ghee. They sat together on the low chowki, eating quietly, talking about small things like the price of vegetables, and Zara's college work, when Ammi looked at Hina and said casually,

"Hina, beta, dress nicely tonight. Wear the new shalwar."

Hina's fork stopped halfway to her mouth.

"Why, Ammi?"

Ammi smiled, folding the flatbread. "An old friend of your father, Kamran (Hina's late father's close friend), saw me in the market the other day. He called yesterday. He says he wants to visit-not just a visit, but he will bring a proposal for you. His son has been in America; he came back last week. They want to finish everything quickly." Hina felt a storm roll through her. Her plate blurred.

A proposal? Now? Her chest felt tight. How could she tell her mother that her heart belonged to Zara's brother? How could she say she could never marry another man when even thinking of it felt like betrayal?

"Ammi," she whispered, "I want to study. Please tell them I cannot accept now."

Ammi's face stayed gentle but firm.

"Beta, you know we cannot refuse a respectable family. Your father would have agreed. This boy is working in America; he will give you a good life there. He is handsome, and well-settled. You are lucky, Hina. Don't say no to blessing."

Hina's throat tightened. She had no proof of Ayzen's heart, no promise from him, and no sign he would ever see her as more than Zara's friend. She felt very small all at once. She went to her room and stood before the mirror. Her dupatta lay over the chair. She touched her face-no makeup, just pink cheeks from crying and the roundness of youth. The image looking back at her was familiar and strange. She cried and cried until her chest ached.

How will I see him with another girl? She thought.

'Why is he so cold? Don't I look pretty? Am I less because I am poor..?' She questioned to herself.

When evening fell, Ammi gave Hina the look that meant there was no choice. Hina dressed in the simple shalwar her mother picked-clean, neat, and a pale colour that suited her. The doorbell rang like a drum in her chest. She walked down slowly, each step meaning more than it should. Even without makeup, even with wet eyes, she looked like the small, brave girl who had always dreamed.

In the sitting room, Kamran (father's friend) rose as she entered, along with his son, Zohaib (the suitor), tall, with a fair complexion that shone under the light. A neatly trimmed beard framed his face, and he sat with a straight, proud posture that told of his self-importance. His clothes were stylish, his manner calm, as though he carried the world in his pocket. Anyone would have said he looked like a "perfect proposal". But to Hina's eyes, he was a shadow compared to Ayzen. He had presence, yes, but not the depth, not the quiet strength that Ayzen carried without trying. Her mother sat straight, smoothing her dupatta with a proud, nervous hand.

"Ma sha Allah, Hina, you have grown into a beautiful young woman," Kamran said warmly.

He had seen her when she was a child, and now he could not believe how she had changed. Polite words went around the room: chai, samosas, and small talk about relatives and weather. But Zohaib, his son, sat quietly, watching Hina as if she were the only thing in the room. His eyes did not leave her. After a while, Kamran smiled.

"Why don't you two step onto the veranda for a little chat? It will make things easier."

The veranda smelt faintly of jasmine and carried the evening breeze. They sat across from each other, the faint noise of the street outside humming in the background. Zohaib leaned forward, his voice smooth, and practiced.

"So, Hina, tell me about your studies, your dreams."

Hina answered in short, careful sentences, her eyes on her lap. She wanted nothing to do with being gentle for him. She kept the truth tucked away: my heart already belongs to someone else. Then, without warning, Zohaib reached out, lifted her chin gently, and said in a low voice,

"Why aren't you looking at me? Look at me, Hina."

The touch burnt like a hot coal. Hina flinched. That small, bold movement deciding her face should meet his felt like an owner taking possession of something he had no right to. Her face went hot, not because of shame, but because of anger that someone could assume any right over her. Her hand rose before her mind caught up. The slap was sharp in the quiet veranda. The sound echoed even outside, where her Ammi and Kamran were speaking.

"How dare you touch me," Hina said, voice shaking but steady. Her eyes burnt. She did not lower them.

Zohaib blinked, surprised, then smiled like a man who enjoyed being defied. His voice was soft, and cruel with confidence.

"You will be mine anyway. When I have you, I will teach you how to respect me."

Inside, her mother's nervous laughter tried to cover the tension. But on the veranda, Hina sat still, every nerve awake. Zohaib's cheek stung faintly, but his pride stung sharper. Before Hina's fire could spread, footsteps approached.

Her mother and Kamran were already on their way, clearly the sharp crack had reached them. Zohaib stood quickly, brushing his kurta and forcing a laugh.

"Oh no, sorry, I slipped against the chair," he said smoothly, pointing to the wooden armrest as if it were guilty. "It made such a sound."

Kamran chuckled, a little relieved.

"Be careful, beta. This old house has tricks."

Ammi also laughed nervously, though her eyes darted between her daughter and Zohaib. The tension in the veranda melted under polite smiles, like spilt water covered quickly with sand. Within minutes, the guests excused themselves. Kamran promised they would return soon to talk further. When the door closed and the house grew quiet, Hina stood frozen. Her hands were still trembling. Her Ammi began gathering empty cups, humming like nothing had happened.

"Ammi..."

Hina finally spoke, her voice low but tight.

"He touched me. He lifted my chin as if... as if I was...."

She broke off, the words choking her. "I slapped him. I couldn't help it."

Her mother paused only a second, then sighed and set the tray down.

"Beta, don't make it into something it isn't. He was only curious. You weren't looking at him, so maybe he just wanted you to. That's all."

Hina's eyes widened. "Ammi, he had no right to do that. I told you...."

Ammi shook her head gently, almost as if soothing a child.

"These things happen, Hina. Men are different. Don't ruin a good proposal with overthinking. He is educated; he is settled in America. You will live a happy life. Forget this small matter."

Hina felt her chest cave in. Her mother's words fell heavier than Zohaib's touch. If even her own mother couldn't see the difference between curiosity and disrespect, who would? She bit her lip, swallowed her pain, and went to her room silently. There, she buried her face in her pillow and cried not just from anger, not just from fear, but from the crushing loneliness of realising no one was standing with her.

A week had passed since that evening on the veranda. Hina tried to focus on her studies, trying to bury the ache in her heart for Ayzen, but it never fully disappeared. She moved through her days quietly, reading, writing, and helping her mother, all while feeling a hollow ache whenever she thought of him. One morning, her Ammi received a call. She picked it up, and Hina could hear the excitement in her voice almost immediately. After a few minutes, she hurried to Hina, eyes shining.

"Beta!" her mother exclaimed, clutching Hina's hands.

"Kamran called. He says... they agreed! Zohaib loves you as his bride, and they want to arrange the wedding as soon as possible! We'll need to start your passport and other documents right away!"

Hina's chest tightened. Her mother's happiness and tears of joy overwhelmed her. Hina could barely respond. Inside, she felt like her heart was breaking all over again. Seeing her mother so elated, she didn't argue. She whispered to herself, Maybe this is my fate...But deep inside, a voice burnt quietly, firmly.

'Zohaib is not the one for me. He touched me without asking, without caring for my feelings. Ayzen... Ayzen never even looked at me that way. That is what makes a man truly worthy.'

Every celebratory smile, and every excited word from her mother felt like a reminder that she could not have the love she truly wanted. Hina nodded silently, letting her tears fall quietly, hidden in the shadow of her forced smile. Her mother, unaware of the storm inside, hugged her tightly.

"Beta, Ma sha Allah! You will have a good life now."

Hina held onto her mother's hands, feeling the warmth, while deep inside, she felt nothing but a quiet, burning ache, a longing that no wealth, no wedding, could ever fill.

A few days passed, and Hina's home had transformed into a whirlwind of activity. Brightly coloured fabric hung in corners, trays of sweets and snacks were arranged on the low table, and her mother moved around with a constant smile, supervising everything. Hina watched quietly, her heart heavy.

"Beta, can you help me with the invitations?" Her mother asked, holding a stack of cards decorated with gold borders. Hina nodded, her hands trembling slightly as she picked them up.

"Ma, do we really have to do all this so quickly?" Hina asked softly, not meeting her mother's eyes.

"Beta, why are you worried? Zohaib is such a good boy. And you'll have a beautiful life. Everything will be perfect," her mother said, adjusting Hina's dupatta as if trying to shield her from any worry.

Hina forced a smile, but inside, she felt a storm. Perfect for him, maybe, but not for me. How can I be happy with someone who thinks lifting my chin and touching me is okay? Her phone buzzed; it was Kamran.

"Hina beta, Zohaib wants to see you tomorrow to discuss some wedding arrangements. Will you be ready?"

His cheerful voice said through the phone.

Hina's heart sank, but she replied politely,

"Yes, Uncle Kamran."

The next day, Zohaib arrived.

"Hi, Hina," Zohaib said, extending his hand. Hina avoided his gaze and nodded.

"Hii," she replied softly, letting her hands rest in her lap.

Her Ammi nudged her slightly. "Beta, please discuss the arrangements with him. He's here to help."

Zohaib began listing things he wanted for the wedding: the catering, the flowers, and the colours for the outfits. Hina listened quietly, making notes, but every time his shoulder touched her shoulder accidentally or leaned too close, she flinched inside.

This is not love... This is control. Ayzen would never do something like this.

During a pause, Hina's cousin whispered to her, "You look so beautiful, Hina. Zohaib is lucky." Hina forced a small smile but thought bitterly'Am I really lucky if my heart isn't in this?

Later, in a quiet moment when her mother went to check on the catering, Hina spoke softly to Zohaib.

"Zohaib, I... I want to be clear. I will respect you and your family, but I need to live my life as I wish. I want my voice to matter too."

She said, her eyes meeting his firmly for the first time. Zohaib's expression softened for a moment, but then he smiled, a little arrogantly. "Of course, Hina. You will have everything you want... as long as you are my bride."

She clenched her hands in her lap, holding back tears. Everything I want... but not my heart. Nothing can fill this empty place but Ayzen. Over the next days, the house was filled with tailors taking measurements, jewellery shops delivering sparkling sets, and relatives checking everything from flower arrangements to the seating plan. Hina moved through it all silently, helping when needed, avoiding unnecessary interactions with Zohaib. She perfected the polite smile that hid the storm in her heart. One evening, while arranging the guest seating with her mother, she whispered,

"Ma, do you think... I will be happy?"

Her mother paused, adjusting a cushion. "Beta, happiness comes in different ways. You will be safe, respected, and cared for. Isn't that enough?"

Hina nodded, but her heart whispered 'No, Ma.' True happiness... true love... is not here. Ayzen is still the one I want, even if he doesn't know it. That night, Hina lay on her bed, staring at the ceiling. The golden lights of the house reflected in her window. She imagined Ayzen's calm eyes, his gentle smile, and the way he never forced anything upon her. Why can't life give me what my heart desires? Maybe I love him this much because he respects me. He knows how a man should be honourable, careful, and strong in his own way, yet gentle with others. He doesn't need to prove anything by controlling or touching... He just exists with dignity. That's why my heart beats for him, not for Zohaib. She sighed, hugging her pillow tightly.

A week more, and she would be Zohaib's bride. A week more and she would step into a world of luxury and expectation but without the one she truly longed for. The wedding preparations continued, everyone around her filled with excitement. But Hina's heart remained in quiet rebellion, silently hoping and waiting for a miracle that might never come.

Chapter 6

It was a bright afternoon. Hina had gone out for shopping with Zohaib. Her heart was heavy; she felt trapped in a life she didn't want, and every smile she forced herself to wear felt like a mask. Zohaib was trying to act cheerful, but his attention kept landing on Hina. The mall was buzzing with people, bright lights reflecting off the glass walls. Hina walked beside Zohaib, her hands clutching her shopping bags a little too tightly. Her heart felt like it was trapped between fear and frustration. Zohaib smiled casually, but his gaze lingered too long.

"Come on, let's take a picture together. Just one, it won't take long," he said, holding out his phone.

Hina shook her head sharply, stepping back. "No, I don't want a picture."

"Why not? Don't be silly," Zohaib said, reaching for her arm.

Hina pulled away, her cheeks burning. "I said no," she repeated, her voice trembling just a little. She felt trapped, exposed, and more alone than ever.

And then... she felt a presence behind her. Calm. Strong. Familiar.

"Hina?" a voice said, concerned.

Her heart skipped. She turned slowly. Ayzen was walking towards her, eyes focused entirely on her. He looked tall and calm, his posture firm, a strength radiating from him. His eyes scanned the scene in seconds, noticing Zohaib's hand on her arm and the discomfort written all over her face. He stepped closer.

"Hina... Is something wrong? Are you in trouble?"

Hina froze. The world seemed to stop. She could barely speak.

"He... he is the man my mother has chosen. The wedding... it's in four days. We came shopping, and he wants a picture together... I don't want it."

Zohaib glared, confused.

"Who are you? Mind your own business."

Ayzen ignored him, his attention fully on Hina. He stepped slightly forward towards Zohaib, voice calm but firm, and said.

"Don't force her. It's not right to make her uncomfortable. Respect her boundaries, or there will be consequences."

Zohaib blinked, caught off guard. He opened his mouth, but Ayzen's steady, unwavering gaze froze him. Hina could see it in his eyes; he was serious and protective, and nothing would stand in his way if she was being hurt. Hina's chest ached. Relief and fear collided inside her. She wanted to run to him, to hide in his presence, yet she knew she couldn't.

"I... I'm okay," she whispered, but her voice trembled, and her hands shook.

Zohaib, still confused and slightly offended, muttered, "Let's go," looking at Hina.

Hina walked with him, but every step felt heavy. She kept glancing back, her eyes meeting Ayzen's once more. For a split second, it felt like the world around them disappeared. Her eyes silently begged him, 'Please protect me. Make me yours.' Ayzen didn't move, but Hina felt the unspoken promise in his gaze, the care and protection she had always dreamed of. Hina's hands trembled slightly as she clutched her shopping bags.

She felt a burning mixture of hope and despair. Hope because Ayzen had noticed her, and had cared enough to protect her even in public. Despair because she was still bound to Zohaib, whose touch had felt like possession rather than care. Her gaze lingered on Ayzen for one last moment as they rounded the corner. His eyes met hers again, and she felt it like a warm, silent promise. He sees me. He understands me. Tears pricked her eyes, but this time they were not just for sadness; they were for the recognition of a love so rare, so honest, that it made her heart ache and hope at the same time.

Chapter 7

That evening, Ayzen's house was alive with chatter, laughter, clinking plates, and the aroma of biryani filling every corner. Everyone in the house was seated around the long dining table, casually talking about Zara's college, family matters, and the latest neighbourhood gossip. Ayzen sat quietly, scrolling through his phone, his mind elsewhere. Suddenly, his father cleared his throat. The room went quiet. All eyes turned toward him. "I think it's time for some happiness in this house," he said warmly, yet the weight of his words hung heavy. The sisters looked at each other, curious.

"What do you mean, Baba?" one asked.

His father smiled faintly, looking at his elder sister.

"Why don't you give your daughter, Anoosha, to Ayzen? It's time he settles down. Keeping the marriage within the family is best, isn't it?"

Ayzen's hand slammed on the table, startling everyone. His face went pale, then red with anger.

"Dad!" he said, voice shaking.

"How can you decide this without asking me?"

His father's gaze sharpened.

"Son... Are you in love with someone else?"

Ayzen's jaw tightened. "No, Baba. I'm not in love. But I have expectations for my wife. Don't decide for me."

With that, he pushed back his chair and left the room, leaving a tense silence. His parents and aunts whispered to Anoosha, encouraging her to charm him, to linger near him, to win his heart. Days passed. Anoosha tried everything, like making him chai, having small talk, and dressing beautifully, but Ayzen remained cold, unmoved, and distant as if nothing could reach him.

Then his father, approaching him in his room, asks a question that stopped him cold.

"Tell me who you will marry, Ayzen. I want to know the reason."

The words echoed in his mind, unfamiliar and heavy. Who... could he say? For the first time, his mind started to drift slowly, unknowingly, towards Hina, the girl who had silently loved him madly and endlessly. Memories flooded back: the way she laughed softly, her kind eyes, her courage, and her unwavering respect for him even when he ignored her. And then he thought of the love he had lost, the girl who had left him before, and the emptiness that had followed. And suddenly, a thought struck him with sharp clarity:

What if Hina is a blessing meant for me? What if this girl, who had always cared quietly, could give him something deeper, something real? But reality hit him hard. She was already promised to another.

Her wedding... it was happening soon. Ayzen felt his chest tighten, a strange mix of longing, regret, and helplessness.

He realised, for the first time, that Hina's love-mad, pure, and unshakeable-was something he could have never ignored. Yet now, time had moved too fast. She was slipping away, and he had no claim, no chance, and no words strong enough to reach her. Ayzen inhaled slowly, his gaze dropping to the floor.

"Baba... I... I need time to think," he said softly, though inside, his heart had already answered.

That night, after the family dinner, Anoosha remembered she had a party the next day. Panic fluttered in her chest; she hadn't picked up her dress from the tailor yet. But a mischievous idea struck her. She ran to her mother.

"Ammi, ask Ayzen to take me to the tailor tonight."

She said with sparkling eyes.

"I can't go alone; I need him to come with me."

Ayzen was relaxing in the living room when his aunt approached him.

"Beta, can you take Anoosha to the tailor? She has to pick up her stitched dress tonight."

He frowned. "I have some work. Ask Zaroon or Hamza to go," he said firmly.

"No, beta," his aunt insisted. "It's better if you go yourself."

Before he could protest further, his mother entered the room, arms folded.

"Ayzen, you will go. Take her," she said firmly.

He sighed, shoulders stiff, muttering, "Fine," though his heart wasn't in it. Anoosha's face lit up. She spent almost an hour trying on dresses, checking herself in every mirror, fussing over every detail to impress him. Ayzen, however, kept glancing at his watch, impatient.

"Are you going to take forever?" He barked, his tone more frustrated than cruel.

Finally, Anoosha ran up to him, twirling in her favourite dress. "How do I look?" she asked, expecting praise. "Mm... fine," Ayzen replied, barely glancing at her, and walked ahead without another word. They reached the tailor shop. The air smelt of fresh fabric and thread, the bell above the door chiming as customers came and went. And there she was, Hina, standing by the counter, delicate and small, five feet tall, lifting her head to glance at him. Ayzen froze. Being six feet tall, his frame casting a shadow, he looked at her with a depth of feeling he had never allowed himself to acknowledge. His chest tightened. His eyes, usually calm and guarded, now glistened, reflecting pain he couldn't hide. What can I do now? He thought. Why does my heart ache seeing her? Why am I feeling this when she is going to be someone else's bride?

Hina watched him for a fleeting moment, her eyes catching the raw emotion in his. Her chest felt like it would collapse. Why is he looking at me like that? She thought. Why now? Then reality hit her like a sharp stone. Her hands trembled.

What brings them together? What if... what if Anoosha and he are getting married?

The thought made her knees weak, her throat tight. She tried to steady herself, but her lips wavered, and tears threatened to spill. Every step she had taken toward this moment, the hope, the longing, now felt like a cruel joke. Ayzen, sensing someone nearby, turned his attention quickly toward a friend who was passing by, speaking politely, trying to cover the turmoil in his chest. Hina, meanwhile, was not alone. Anoosha saw the perfect opportunity. She approached Hina, her voice sweet but mocking.

"So... you see, Hina?" Anoosha said, tilting her head, a smirk playing on her lips. "You can never be his bride. Ayzen himself... has chosen me. Can you believe it? He's going to be mine. Isn't that wonderful?" Hina felt as if the floor had fallen beneath her. She wanted to speak, to protest, but her throat was dry. Her chest ached unbearably. Anoosha, sensing Hina's pain, sauntered closer with a smirk that seemed designed to cut through Hina's heart.

"Oh, Hina," she said softly, mockingly, "I can see it in your face. You know... Very soon, you'll be someone else's bride. And he..." She tilted her head toward Ayzen, who was speaking to a friend. "...he's mine. Ayzen chose me himself. Isn't that exciting?"

Hina felt her knees weaken. She tried to steady herself, but the words struck her like blows. Chosen... mine... she repeated in her head, each syllable burning her inside. The reality of her own impending wedding, coupled with seeing Ayzen's protective gaze, made her feel like her heart was being ripped apart. Anoosha laughed lightly, the sound cruel and tinkling. "Enjoy your last days, Hina. Soon, it won't be him you see every day... It'll be someone else holding your hand. You'll smile, but you'll always know... he wasn't yours." Hina forced a calm smile, masking the storm raging within. Inside, her heart was breaking, her dreams of him slipping further away. Yet, as she turned to leave, she caught one last look from Ayzen. That fleeting glance ignited a small, painful flame of hope and longing inside her before reality crashed down again.

At Hina's house the wedding celebrations had already begun. The house was full of noise, laughter, and the sound of dhol beating in the background. Relatives moved around decorating the place, some carrying trays of sweets, others busy arranging flowers. Outside, children ran with sparklers in their hands. The air was filled with joy. But on the other side, away from the noise, Hina sat quietly in her room. Her hands trembled as she folded her dupatta neatly on the bed. Her eyes were red from crying, though she quickly wiped her tears each time someone walked in. She didn't want anyone to notice her pain-not her mother, not her cousins, not even Zara.

That evening, she dialled Zara's number. When Zara picked up, Hina's voice broke.

"Zara...How are you...? I just wanted to say... I'll miss Ayzen so much. I know he never loved me. But I did. And I'll always remember him. He was... everything to me, even if I wasn't anything to him." Her breath shook, and for a moment, silence filled the line. Then Hina continued softly, her voice heavy with tears.

"And Zara... if you ever see Ayzen feeling down, if he ever forgets his worth, tell him... Tell him how much I loved him. Tell him he was strong, and he was always enough. I couldn't be his, but at least let him know what he meant to me. I wish him all the happiness in the world. Always. Zara. Always."

On the other end, Zara's eyes filled with tears. She pressed her lips together, unable to reply, her chest heavy with the weight of Hina's words. She kept quiet. She didn't know what to say.

Hina took a deep breath and continued softly,

"But it's okay. This is my fate. I'll accept it. I'll try to move on. And I'll try to be happy with Zohaib. I don't want to upset Ammi anymore. She just wants to see me smiling." She ended the call with that. That night she slept with the thought that tomorrow would be a new life for her.

'Sometimes, life doesn't break you to hurt you; it breaks you to redirect you and what is not written for you will never be yours, even if the whole world tries to place it in your hands.'

The wedding day arrived. The hall glittered with lights, with flowers hanging from every corner and the stage decorated in red and gold. The sound of laughter echoed everywhere; women in colourful clothes moved about, serving guests and greeting each other. In her room, Hina was dressed like a bride. The red bridal dress hugged her shoulders, her hands full of mehndi, bangles clinking softly with every movement. Her mother adjusted her dupatta with teary eyes.

"You look so beautiful, Hina," she whispered, kissing her forehead.

Finally, the moment arrived. The hall grew quiet as Hina was called forward. Her mother held her hand gently, guiding her towards the stage. The sound of her anklets echoed softly with each step, blending with the distant murmur of guests. Hina walked slowly; each step felt like a step away from her dreams and a step towards her fate. The red bridal lehenga shimmered under the golden lights, embroidered with delicate patterns that caught every sparkle. A long dupatta was draped over her head, falling gracefully to her hands.

Her eyes, lined with kohl, seemed deeper than ever, like they carried a thousand unspoken stories.

Zohaib, already seated on the stage, straightened proudly when he saw her. His sherwani, gold and ivory, made him look like a man ready to conquer the world. But when his eyes met hers, his expression softened. His gaze travelled from the glittering jewellery on her neck to the soft blush on her cheeks. He smiled, a satisfied smile, like he had won a treasure that belonged only to him. The hall seemed to fade for him; he only saw her.

The bride who was about to become his. Guests whispered in admiration as Hina walked. Some praised her beauty; others smiled with joy. But inside her, every step carried the pain she could not show. As she reached the stage, her mother gently placed her beside Zohaib. The two now sat side by side, the bride and groom, the centre of everyone's attention.

Zohaib leaned slightly, his voice low but filled with pride.

"You look perfect, Hina. Just perfect."

Hina forced a faint smile. Her heart was burning, but her lips smiled as if she agreed. The imam came forward with the nikah papers. The guests leaned closer. The hall grew quieter, waiting for the sacred words that would make them husband and wife. The imam adjusted his glasses, cleared his throat, and began to read in a steady, respectful voice.

"This is the nikah between Zohaib Ahmed, son of Kamran Ahmed, and Hina Fatima, daughter of the late Irfan Malik..."

Every word echoed in the silent hall. The pen in the imam's hand rested on the paper, waiting. Guests held their breaths, their eyes fixed on the stage.

Some women dabbed their eyes with dupatta, whispering prayers. Men nodded, their faces serious with the weight of the moment. The imam then looked at Zohaib and said.

"Zohaib Ahmed, son of Kamran Ahmed, do you accept this nikah with Hina Fatima, daughter of the late Irfan Malik, with the mehr settled upon?"

Zohaib's lip curved into a small smile; he looks at Hina and takes a deep breath. His voice was confident, almost proud. And says,

"Qubool hai." (I accept.)

The imam repeated again, as tradition requires.

"Zohaib Ahmed, son of Kamran Ahmed, do you accept this nikah with Hina Fatima?"

Again, Zohaib's voice rang out.

"Qubool hai."

For the third and final time, the imam asked.

"Zohaib Ahmed, son of Kamran Ahmed, do you accept this nikah with Hina Fatima?"

Zohaib leaned slightly forward, his eyes on Hina as he spoke louder.

"Qubool hai."

The guests let out soft murmurs of approval, a few smiles breaking out. Zohaib looked satisfied, ready to sign, his chest swelling with pride. The imam's eyes now turned to Hina, who sat quietly beside him. The hall was so still; even the sound of her breath seemed loud. All eyes moved to the bride, waiting for her voice.

"Hina Fatima, daughter of the late Irfan Malik..." The imam said gently, "Do you accept this nikah with Zohaib Ahmed, son of Kamran Ahmed, with the mehr agreed upon?"

The entire hall leaned closer, waiting for her reply...The words fell into the silence. Everyone turned their eyes to her. The weight of the moment pressed down on her chest. Hina lowered her gaze. Her hands trembled in her lap. For a second, she couldn't breathe. Memories rushed through. Ayzen's face, his silence, his indifference, her countless prayers for his love. A part of her heart screamed, won't he at least come now? Won't he stop this? But there was no Ayzen. There were only her mother's anxious eyes, silently begging her to be strong. With a shaky breath, Hina lifted her eyes towards her mother, then to the imam. Her voice quivered, but she forced the words out.

"Qubool hai..."

The imam nodded once and then repeated again.

'Hina Fatima, daughter of the late Irfan Malik...Do you accept this nikah with Zohaib Ahmed, son of Kamran Ahmed, with the mehr agreed upon?'

Her lips pressed together. For a moment she almost broke down, but then she whispered again,

"Qubool hai..."

The crowd relaxed slightly; some guests smiled. Zohaib leaned back, satisfied, his eyes shining with pride. Hina kept her eyes lowered, her heart heavy. The imam opened again and asked the same question.

'Hina Fatima, daughter of the late Irfan Malik...Do you accept this nikah with Zohaib Ahmed, son of Kamran Ahmed, with the mehr agreed upon?

Chapter 8

Hina's hands shivered in her lap. Her eyes filled with tears, blurring the paper in front of her. She lowered her gaze, afraid her emotions would betray her. Slowly, with her fingertips, she brushed away the tears before anyone could see. A deep breath escaped her lips. Her heart pounded against her chest as if begging her not to say it. She looked at her mother, who nodded softly, eyes hopeful yet heavy with unspoken prayers. Then Hina turned back to the imam, lips parting to whisper the words "Qubool hai", and then.....

SLAP!

The sound cracked through the hall like thunder. The mic picked it up, echoing sharply. Everyone froze. Pin-drop silence fell instantly, as if the entire room had stopped breathing. Guests turned in shock, chairs creaked, and whispers died mid-air. All eyes darted to the front of the stage. Zohaib was holding his cheek, red and stinging from the force of the slap. His expression was a mixture of anger, shock, and shame. He stood frozen, unable to react, as if the ground beneath him had vanished. Hina's eyes widened. Her heart skipped. She turned slowly, following the eyes of the crowd, only to see a woman standing there, her chest rising and falling with rage. She wasn't shaking with fear; she was trembling with fury. Tears burnt in her eyes, but her voice was firm as she glared at Zohaib.

She pointed straight at Zohaib, her voice cutting through the silence.

"This man..." she said bitterly, "...is already married to me."

Gasps erupted across the hall. The women at the back covered their mouths, men shifted in their seats, and children clung to their mothers. All eyes were locked on her. Zohaib's face drained of colour. He opened his mouth to speak, but no words came out. He was caught like a thief caught in the light. The woman didn't stop. Her voice broke, but her anger pushed her forward.

"While in America, he promised me love. He married me. He swore I was his only one. And now he sits here, ready to marry another girl, as if I never existed!" She reached into her handbag and pulled out her phone, unlocking it with trembling fingers. She raised the screen high enough for everyone to see. There were pictures of her and Zohaib together, laughing, standing close, holding each other in ways no stranger could deny. The hall buzzed with shock. Murmurs rippled through the crowd like a wave. Hina's chest tightened. She felt as though the ground beneath her was slipping away. Her eyes filled with tears as she stared at the images. Her lips trembled. The woman turned to her, voice softening but still strong.

"Don't marry him. Don't make the mistake I made. He will cheat you too."

The imam lowered his head, his voice lost, and his hand quietly closed the nikah papers.

Hina's mother broke into tears, her dupatta slipping from her head as she sobbed into her hands. The relatives whispered louder now, some shaking their heads, others glaring at Zohaib. Zohaib tried to speak, stammering...

"She's lying, Hina... don't listen to..." but, his voice cracked; his confidence was gone.

Hina stood slowly, her bridal bangles jingling, her lehenga rustling as she rose. Tears streamed down her cheeks. She turned toward her mother, voice breaking but firm.

"Ammi... I told you. I told you he wasn't right for me. I felt it... and see now it's true."

'Not all broken promises are tragedies;
Some are the turning points we did not know we needed.'

Her words silenced even the whispers. Zohaib's father stood suddenly, his face red with rage. He walked up to the stage and slapped his son hard across the face. "Shame on you!" he shouted. The sound echoed in the hall once again. Zohaib stumbled back, his pride shattered. His father's hand still trembled with fury as he pointed to the door. "Get out of here before I disown you!" Zohaib lowered his head, unable to face anyone, and hurried out of the hall. The woman who had exposed him stood breathing heavily, tears running down her face. She looked once at Hina and hugged her tightly. The hall was heavy with silence. All eyes fell on Hina, her bridal dress glittering under the lights, but her face pale and broken. Her mother hugged her, crying into her shoulder.

And in that moment, everyone was asking the same question her mother voiced aloud through her tears:

"Now... who will marry my daughter?"

The moment Zara realised what had happened, she didn't waste a second. She dialled her brother's number, her voice trembling as she spoke.

"Hina's wedding... It's broken, Bhai. She's crying... You need to come!"

Ayzen's heart skipped. Without another word, he cut the call, grabbed his car keys, and rushed out. His car sped through the streets; every second felt endless. His breathing was heavy, his mind focused only on Hina. When he reached the wedding hall, he barely paused. Zara met him at the entrance.

"Bhai, it's all messed up. Hina... she..."

Ayzen didn't wait. He walked through the crowd, his eyes locking on Hina. She stood there in her bridal dress, stunning beyond words. Her cheeks were slightly pink from crying, her eyes still glistening, but she looked ethereal, like a dream he had finally caught sight of. For a heartbeat, he simply admired her beauty. Then, without a single word to Hina, he turned to her mother. His voice was firm, carrying a determination that left no doubt.

"Ammi, I am ready to marry your daughter. I really want to marry Hina. I would love to make her my better half and complete my deen with her."

Hina's mother's eyes widened, her hands clutching her dupatta. "Beta... I can't thank you enough. You've saved our respect... and my daughter."

Tears of relief and joy ran down her face as she led Ayzen closer to Hina. Turning to Hina, she asked softly,

"Hina... would you like to marry Ayzen? He has chosen to marry you." Hina's heart raced. She could barely believe her eyes. The love she had longed for, the one she had dreamt of silently, was here. This was not a dream. Trembling, she whispered,

"Yes, Ammi..."

She slowly lifted her gaze and met Ayzen's eyes. He looked at her with a gentle smile, and in that moment, her entire world seemed to stop.

"Save it for later, Hina," he said softly, making her cheeks burn with shyness and happiness. Now Ayzen sat beside Hina, his hand close to hers, ready to become her groom. The hall fell completely silent. The imam, holding the nikah papers, looked at the couple, his voice steady and soft, yet carrying the weight of the sacred moment.

'Hina Fatima, daughter of the late Irfan Malik...Do you accept this nikah with Ayzen Ahmed, son of Yazeen Rahim, with the mehr agreed upon?'

Ayzen's gaze met Hina's. His eyes softened, full of relief and unspoken promises. A small, shy smile tugged at his lips. With a steady breath, he whispered, "Qubool hai." The imam nodded and turned to Hina.

'Hina Fatima, daughter of the late Irfan Malik..." The imam said gently, "Do you accept this nikah with Ayzen Ahmed, son of Yazeen Rahim, with the mehr agreed upon?'

Hina lifted her eyes to meet his. In that instant, all her past heartaches, doubts, and longings seemed to melt away. Her lips gave a gentle smile, her heart full of warmth and hope. "Qubool hai," she said softly, her voice carrying the weight of her feelings. The imam repeated the question once more, as is tradition, ensuring the commitment was sincere. Again, Ayzen and Hina looked into each other's eyes. There was no hesitation now, only love, understanding, and a shared promise of a life ahead. "Qubool hai," they said together, their voices in harmony, filling the hall with a quiet, joyful energy. Time seemed to pause. Guests leaned forward, eyes glimmering with happiness, witnessing the beginning of something sacred. Their hands almost brushed, hearts racing, a silent acknowledgement passing between them that this was theirs, a love they had finally claimed.

Ayzen stood up slowly and reached for Hina's hand. She looked up, her eyes wide with surprise and happiness. He gently held her hand, helping her rise beside him. The hall seemed to fade around them as he pulled her into a warm, protective hug. Hina could hear the steady beat of his heart. For the first time, it felt like everything she had ever longed for had come true. Her chest lifted with relief, and tears of joy pricked her eyes.

"I know how much you love me," Ayzen whispered softly into her ear, his voice calm but full of emotion. "And I love you even more. You will never cry again... I will always be there for you." Hina rested her head briefly against his chest, her tears slipping quietly. A soft smile appeared on her lips as she whispered,

"I know... and that's why I loved you so much."

Hina's mother cleared her throat, a gentle signal that it was time to step back. They slowly pulled apart, hands still entwined. Zara stood nearby, her eyes glistening with tears of joy. She watched her brother finally find the true love he deserved and saw her best friend's prayers being answered in the most beautiful way. Her heart swelled with happiness for both of them. And Zara quickly walked over, a playful smile on her face, teasing them softly.

"Finally! Took you two long enough," she laughed, clicking pictures of them together. Hina couldn't help but giggle, her cheeks warming. Ayzen gave her a small, shy smile, brushing a strand of hair from her face. For a moment, the world felt perfect. Then reality slowly crept in. As they looked around, they realised how the family might react. His family, who had always shown coldness toward Hina-would they ever accept her now? How would they explain this sudden turn of events? Ayzen's jaw tightened slightly, a flicker of worry crossing his face. Hina noticed, her fingers squeezing his hand reassuringly.

"We'll face it together," she whispered. The guests, unaware of the inner thoughts of the newlyweds, began moving toward the dining area. Laughter, chatter, and the aroma of rich food filled the hall as everyone prepared to enjoy the wedding feast. Zara nudged them gently.

"Come on, lovebirds. Let's eat before all the good dishes are gone."

She teased, grinning. Hina and Ayzen exchanged a glance, with smiles on their lips, knowing that while this moment was perfect, the challenges ahead would need courage, patience, and love to overcome.

'What is written for you will reach you, even if the whole world stands against it.'

Together, they started walking down the aisle. Each step felt heavy yet magical. Guests leaned forward, some whispering congratulations, others smiling warmly. Hina's bridal gown shimmered under the hall lights. She could feel Ayzen's steady presence beside her, the protective aura surrounding her. For a moment, she let herself breathe in the reality that they were husband and wife now. Zara ran ahead slightly, clicking pictures and capturing every smile and shy glance. Hina felt a surge of happiness seeing her best friend so happy for her. Yet a small worry lingered:

How would Ayzen's family react? Would they accept her?

Hina hugged her mother slowly, burying her face in Ammi's shoulder. Tears streamed down both their faces, the weight of the day pressing softly on them. "Beta", her mother whispered, stroking her hair gently, "your husband's house is your house too. Always be patient, treat everyone with respect, be kind, do your work diligently, and be a blessing to him. You are blessed with a good man; never forget that."

Hina nodded, choking back sobs, feeling both the loss of her childhood home and the warmth of her mother's love. With one last squeeze, she pulled away and waved goodbye, tears still glistening in her eyes. Outside, Ayzen opened the car door for her. She stepped in, pausing for a moment to look at him. His calm, protective demeanour and the care in his eyes made her heart swell. For the first time, she felt like a true princess, not just in appearance but in her heart. Memories flashed of the day she first got into his car, the spark that had set her heart alight. And now, she was getting in again, this time as his wife. How beautifully her fate had unfolded,

She thought, overwhelmed with gratitude. Zara climbed into the backseat, her laughter breaking the quiet tension. Ayzen settled behind the wheel, giving Hina a small, knowing smile as he started the car. The three of them drove toward Ayzen's home, hearts full but minds anxious. None of them knew how his family would react, yet for now, Hina felt secure in the warmth of Ayzen's presence, ready to face whatever came next.

Chapter 9

The car slowed in front of Ayzen's house. Zara stepped out first, her eyes scanning the home, already anticipating the chaos that was about to unfold. There's going to be a Great War... she thought, shaking her head slightly. Ayzen followed, holding Hina's hand firmly. The front door opened, and the warm smell of home-cooked food and chatter greeted them. The family had just finished dinner, sitting around the table, talking and laughing.

"Aah, beta! You're home! Come, have your dinner!" Ayzen's father called cheerfully.

His mother's eyes narrowed as she turned toward him.

"Where have you both been?" she asked sharply. Then her gaze shifted to Zara. "And you... how was the wedding?"

Ayzen stepped forward confidently, pulling Hina's hand gently. Hina walked beside him, holding his arm, trying to keep her face calm but cheeks flushed. The room went silent as everyone registered their presence. And then... Anoosha appeared. Her face twisted in fury. She ran towards Hina, hand raised, ready to slap her. Ayzen moved like lightning, stepping in front of Hina. His hand pushed Anoosha back firmly. "Stop!" he said, his voice deadly serious.

"I have married Hina. She is my wife. Everyone here must respect that. No one here is allowed to raise a finger against her or question her."

Shock froze the room. Ayzen's mother stared wide-eyed, tears forming as her voice trembled.

"Why... why did you marry this girl? And what about Anoosha? Did you not think about us even for a second?"

She turned to Hina, her tone dripping with anger. "Shameless girl! You got what you wanted!"

Ayzen stepped forward and hugged his mother gently. "Ammi, calm down. It's my life. I had to make a choice. I love her; I cannot see her in pain. Please... at least accept her for me."

Then, without another word, Ayzen looked at Hina. He scooped her up effortlessly, holding her close as he carried her to the bedroom. Hina blushed, her hands lightly touching his shoulders.

"Put me down! Everyone is looking!" she whispered, heart racing.

"You're my wife, meri jaan," Ayzen said with a small, teasing smile. "Don't forget it. You're mine now."

Behind them, Anoosha seethed, her jealousy and anger burning hotter with every step they took. The family erupted into shouting and arguments, Zara explaining to Aleeza what had happened, some trying to protest, others shocked into silence, but Ayzen's focus never wavered. He was determined: no one would hurt Hina. Inside the bedroom, Hina's hands trembled slightly as she realised the reality of the moment. She was finally safe, finally loved, and finally with the man who had always owned her heart.

The celebrations had finally ended, and the house had grown quiet. Hina sat on the edge of the bed, her red bridal veil still draped over her face. Her hands shivered slightly, not from fear, but from the overwhelming thought that she now belonged to him, and he belonged to her. Her heart raced with a mix of excitement, relief, and a hint of shyness she couldn't hide. Ayzen stepped inside, tall and confident, yet for the first time, he felt a flutter of nervousness. His usual steady steps slowed as he saw her sitting there so delicate, so graceful, and framed by the soft glow of the bedroom lights.

He closed the door gently behind him and walked closer. Hina could feel his presence strong, warm, and comforting, and her breath caught in her chest. He sat down across from her, lowering his voice so only she could hear.

"Hina..." he said softly.

Her name on his lips sounded different, like something precious, something he had waited for all his life. She lifted her eyes slowly, just enough for him to catch the shimmer of tears she had not yet wiped away.

"Why are you crying, love?" he asked gently, his voice almost breaking. "This is the happiest day of your life... and mine too."

She tried to smile, her lips trembling. "These are not sad tears. They're... prayers answered."

Ayzen reached out, his fingers brushing hers as he carefully lifted the veil away. For the first time, he saw her face fully, his wife soft, radiant, and breathtaking. He stared for a long moment, silent, memorising every detail as if imprinting it in his heart. "You are beautiful," he whispered, his deep voice filled with awe. "So beautiful." Hina lowered her eyes again, cheeks blushing. Her heart thudded in her chest, with a small, happy smile on her lips. He moved closer, gently taking her trembling hands into his.

"I want to promise you something," he said, looking into her eyes with sincerity. "From today, you are mine, and I am yours. I'll protect you, respect you, and I'll never let these hands feel lonely again." And he kisses her hand. Her eyes filled with tears once more. Ayzen leaned forward slowly, carefully cupping her face in his hands. He pressed a soft, lingering kiss to her forehead.

"Meri jaan," he whispered against her skin, "if ever tears fall from your eyes again, let them only be from happiness." Hina closed her eyes, her heart finally at peace. All the distance, all the heartbreak, every longing she had carried everything had led to this moment. Destiny had brought them together. He didn't pull away. Instead, he wrapped his arms fully around Hina, holding her close to his chest.

She could feel the warmth of his body, the steady rise and fall of his breathing, and the strong rhythm of his heartbeat beneath her ear. Each beat seemed to whisper silently, You are mine... you are mine... you are mine...

Hina rested her head on his chest, letting herself melt into the comfort and safety of his embrace. Her hands instinctively went around his waist, holding him tightly, as if this hug could make the world pause for just a moment. She could feel every inch of him, the steady strength in his back, the gentle pressure of his arms, and the faint scent of his cologne it all felt so familiar yet so new, like a dream come true. Ayzen then leaned his head against hers, pressing his cheek softly to the top of her head. He closed his eyes for a moment, savouring the closeness, the warmth, and the feeling of finally having her in his arms. Slowly, she whispered, looking at him, "I've waited for this... for you... for us..." Hina felt a tear slip down her cheek, not of sadness but of relief and overwhelming happiness. He tilted his head slightly, letting her feel his emotion, and whispered back softly, "Maybe I prayed for you without even realising." They stayed like that for several minutes, simply holding each other, breathing together, letting the world fade away. It was a quiet intimacy that needed no words, just the fact that they were finally together, safe in each other's hearts.

Then, gently, Ayzen lifted her chin with one hand, looking deep into her eyes. Hina felt the promise in it, and her heart swelled with love. He brushed a strand of hair behind her ear and murmured,

"You'll never cry alone again. I'll always be here."

Hina gave a small, shy smile, and she whispered, "I know... that's why I admired you so much."

And once again, Ayzen pulled her closer, holding her as if he could shield her from everything in the world, while Hina rested against him.

The next morning, sunlight spilt softly through the bedroom curtains. Hina stirred awake, her heart still fluttering from the night before. She glanced at Ayzen sleeping peacefully beside her, his strong, broad frame relaxed and calm. A soft smile touched her lips. He looked so... manly, so protective, so hers. Quietly, she dressed in a simple, elegant outfit, taking care not to wake him. Once ready, she leaned down and gently caressed his head.

"Ayzen... Wake up!" She whispered softly.

His eyelids fluttered open, and he blinked against the morning light. When his eyes met hers, with a small smile on his lips. He says, "You're already up?" he asked, his voice still husky from sleep. "Yeah," she replied with a gentle nod, bringing a tray with chai. Ayzen freshened up quickly, sipping the tea, and a warm smile spread across his face as he looked at her.

Just then, there was a knock at the door. Zara and Aleeza entered, their faces bright with excitement.

"Hina! Good morning!" Zara exclaimed. "How's my best friend?"

Hina laughed softly, brushing a strand of hair behind her ear. "Good morning! Everything's fine... just adjusting to my new life."

Aleeza grinned. “So, did he wake up like a prince, or did you have to drag him out of bed?”

“He’s a prince,” Hina said, smiling.

They all laughed, spending a few moments in light conversation, giggling and teasing one another about marriage life. Later, Ayzen led Hina to the breakfast table. His aunt and cousins were already seated, and their eyes flicked toward her with subtle, sharp glances.

“Wow, you look... different today,” one of his cousins said, smiling faintly. “Not that we expected much, you know, from where you come...” Hina kept her smile, calm and polite, her hands folded in her lap. Ayzen noticed the slight tension, and his eyes softened. He reached over, scooping some food onto her plate.

“Here, eat. Don’t mind them,” he said quietly. Everyone had their breakfast. Ayzen had to go out for some work. He looks at Hina, leans, and places a gentle kiss on her forehead. “I’ll come back with a surprise for you later,” he whispered, before leaving the house. Hina spent the morning chatting with Zara and Aleeza, sipping tea, and enjoying small laughs together. Soon, her mother-in-law entered with a serious expression on her face. “So...You got what you wanted finally,” she began, her tone testing and sharp.

“Since you come from a different background and don’t know about this lifestyle, learn to handle this house... and respect our ways.” Hina smiled politely, keeping her tone calm. “Of course, Aunty. I will do my best.” Zara frowned slightly. “Don’t you even want to stand up for yourself?”

Hina shook her head gently. “She is like a mother to me. I know she’s hurt seeing Ayzen marry me suddenly. That’s okay... I respect her feelings.”

Evening fell, painting the sky in soft shades of orange and pink. Hina sat in the living room, her heart unusually light. Suddenly, the sound of a car horn echoed from outside yes, it was Ayzen's car. Her heart skipped, and without thinking, she jumped up, a big smile spreading across her face. She ran to the front door, her dupatta flying behind her, and peeked out just as he stepped out of the car. Ayzen's sharp eyes caught hers for a brief moment.

"Hina," he called gently. She felt her cheeks blushing as she opened the gate, letting him in. Minutes later, he led Hina to the balcony. "Close your eyes," he said softly. Hina obeyed, smiling curiously. He took a small box and lifted her hand gently, sliding a ring onto her finger. Hina opened her eyes and gasped softly. "Thank you... it's beautiful," she said, her voice full of emotion. He smiled, brushing a lock of hair from her face. "Not more than you," he whispered. For a moment, they just stood there, hands intertwined, hearts beating together, the warm glow of the evening wrapping around them like a promise of love, patience, and devotion.

Hina had only been in Ayzen's house a few days, yet it already felt like she was walking on thin glass. His aunts and cousins found small ways to remind her she didn't belong: whispers at the breakfast table, glances exchanged when she walked into the room, and backhanded compliments that stung more than insults. But Hina chose silence over confrontation. Every time she heard a taunt, she reminded herself of her mother's advice: patience, kindness, and respect will always win hearts. So instead of letting the bitterness touch her, she poured her energy into small acts: helping in the kitchen, serving tea, and folding laundry without being asked. And whenever Ayzen caught her eyes from across the room, she saw the reassurance there, like his gaze was telling her` you are not alone.

One evening, as they sat in the living room, Zara leaned closer to her best friend. "Hina, why don't you join college again?" she suggested, her eyes shining with excitement. "You can still finish your studies. You shouldn't give up on your dreams just because you're married." Hina hesitated. "Do you really think I can? With everything going on..."

"Of course," Zara pressed. "Ask Ayzen. I'm sure he'll agree."

Hina turned to him nervously. Ayzen was sitting nearby, scrolling through his phone, but the moment he heard his name, he looked up. "What is it?" he asked warmly.

"Zara says... I should join college again," Hina said softly, almost afraid of the answer. Ayzen gave a smile, and without a second thought, he replied, "Of course you should. Why would I ever stop you from growing?

I'll support you in everything, Hina." Her eyes lit up, her heart swelling with gratitude. Zara clapped her hands happily.

The very next morning, Ayzen dropped them both off at the college gates. Hina stood there, her bag hanging from her shoulder, the sun lighting her face. She looked at the building with a nervous but hopeful heart; it felt like a second chance. Before leaving for work, Ayzen leaned from the car window and said,

"Good luck, Mrs Ayzen. Make me proud." He winked, and Hina couldn't help but smile back, feeling stronger than ever.

Later that evening, Anoosha sat curled up on the sofa, pretending to scroll through her phone, though her eyes were fixed on the couple across the room. Ayzen was sitting near Hina, asking her how her first day at college had gone. His tone was soft, his attention fully hers, and when Hina spoke, her face lit up in a shy smile that made something twist painfully inside Anoosha.

That should have been her smile.

That should have been her place.

Anoosha's grip on her phone tightened until her knuckles turned white. For years, she had imagined being the perfect match for Ayzen-educated, confident, from the same world as him. She had dreamt of wearing the ring Hina now wore, of being the one sitting in his car.

And yet here was this simple, small-town girl, sitting there like she belonged, like she had earned this life. When Ayzen finally left for work, Anoosha followed Hina into the kitchen, her heels clicking sharply against the floor. "So", she said casually, picking up an apple from the counter, "back to college, huh?"

Hina turned, startled, then nodded politely. "Yes... Ayzen thought it would be good for me."

Anoosha smirked, biting into the apple with a loud crunch. "Of course he did. Trying to turn you into the perfect wife, isn't he?"

Hina's fingers froze around the cup she was rinsing. She didn't reply, just lowered her gaze and went back to her work. Anoosha stepped closer, her voice softening into a whisper. "Enjoy this attention while it lasts, Hina. Men like Ayzen... they don't stay interested forever. One day, he'll get bored, and then you'll see where you really stand." Hina swallowed hard, forcing her tears back. Her mother's words echoed in her mind: *patience, kindness, and respect will always win hearts.* She forced herself to stay calm, to not answer back, but inside her chest, her heart felt like it was being squeezed.

From that day, Hina began to feel the change in the air. The house felt colder. Anoosha's words followed her like shadows. Each word stung like a needle. At night, when Ayzen returned home, Hina would force a smile, not wanting him to see the storm inside her. She didn't tell him about Anoosha's talks. She didn't want to burden him or make him feel torn between her and his family.

Chapter 10

It started with a whisper.

Anoosha had overheard it first-a hushed conversation between her mom and aunt in the courtyard. "Did you hear? Mahnoor is back in town. Poor girl, her marriage didn't work out."

"Hmm. And to think she left Ayzen for that man. Fate has a strange way of humbling people." Anoosha's lips curled into a slow smile. That evening, she stood at her mirror, brushing her hair with deliberate calm. In her mind, a plan was already taking shape, one that would place a crack between Hina and Ayzen so wide it would be impossible to ignore.

The next morning, she waited until Ayzen had returned from work and Hina was quietly folding laundry in the corner. Anoosha strolled casually into the living room, her tone deliberately light.

"Oh, Ayzen, guess who's back?"

He looked up from his phone, distracted. "Who?"

"Mahnoor," Anoosha said with a small, knowing smile. "I heard she's divorced now... Poor thing. Must be hard, starting over."

For the briefest moment, something flickered in Ayzen's eyes-a memory, perhaps, or an ache that had never fully healed. He quickly masked it with a neutral expression, but Hina caught it. She saw the slight tightening of his jaw, the way his fingers paused over the screen of his phone.

"Hmm," was all he said before standing up and leaving the room. Hina's heart sank. She stared down at the neatly folded dupatta in her lap, her chest tight with something she didn't fully understand. Anoosha's eyes followed Ayzen as he walked away, then shifted to Hina.

"Oh, don't look so worried," she said sweetly. "I'm sure he's just... surprised. After all, Mahnoor was his first love, wasn't she?"

'Hatred is a fire we light ourselves, hoping it will burn another, but it only scorches our own hands.'

Hina's hands stilled completely. "His... first love?" she asked, barely above a whisper. Anoosha's smile widened. She leaned in slightly, her voice low, as though sharing a precious secret.

"Everyone knows about it, Hina. Before you came along, Mahnoor was the one he was going to marry. She broke his heart when she left. Maybe now that she's back..." She let the words trail off, pretending to shrug, and walked away, leaving her sentence and poison hanging in the air. That night, Hina lay awake, staring at the ceiling. Every sound in the house seemed louder than usual; every passing car made her heart jolt. She thought about Mahnoor, beautiful, confident, belonging to Ayzen's world, and about herself, the girl who always had to fight to prove she belonged here.

The next day, Hina watched Ayzen more closely than usual. When his phone buzzed during dinner and he excused himself to answer it, a wave of dread washed over her. Was it Mahnoor? Was she reaching out to him? She tried to bury the thoughts, but they clung to her like thorns. And Anoosha watched from a distance, her eyes glinting with satisfaction that she just had begun.

That night, Ayzen sat in his study, his tie loosened, files spread across the desk. The soft glow of the lamp lit his sharp features when suddenly his phone buzzed.

'An unknown number.' He frowned, hesitated, and then answered. "Hello?"

The voice on the other end made him freeze.

"Ayzen..."

His grip on the phone tightened. It had been years since he heard that voice. "Mahnoor?" he asked quietly, unable to hide the edge in his tone. "Yes. I... I need to see you. Please meet me tomorrow at the café near the market. I know you hate me for what I did, but please, just for once." Ayzen's jaw clenched. The memories of her betrayal came back like a storm: her laughter with someone else and the way she had walked away, leaving him with nothing but a scar. "No, Mahnoor," he said firmly and cut the call before she could say another word. He leaned back in his chair, staring at the ceiling, his chest rising and falling heavily. For a long moment, he stayed there, as if fighting a battle inside himself.

The next day, Mahnoor stood in front of her mirror, her hands trembling as she put on her favourite red silk kurta. She took her time applying eyeliner, the black kohl tracing her eyes just right, her lips painted with a soft rose tint. She fastened her delicate earrings and took one last look at herself. She had once been Ayzen's everything, and today she needed to remind him of that. Her heart pounded as she entered his office building. She walks to the receptionist and asks if she can meet Ayzen.

"Ayzen is busy," the receptionist said hesitantly.

"I'll wait," Mahnoor replied, her voice steady though her palms were damp with nervousness.

Minutes later, Ayzen stepped out of his cabin. His face hardened when he saw her standing there, as if the past had suddenly walked into the present. "Mahnoor," he said flatly. She smiled faintly. "I had to see you. Please, just five minutes." With a tired sigh, Ayzen gestured for her to follow him inside. Mahnoor stepped into his office, her eyes scanning the space. The dark wood shelves, files arranged with precision, the faint smell of coffee, staff around, meetings going on in other rooms. She thinks to herself, 'so, he is actually so rich.'

"You look different," she said softly as she sat down.

"I am different," Ayzen replied coolly, leaning against the desk. "Why are you here?"

Mahnoor's eyes filled with tears. "Because I have no one else. I made a mistake, Ayzen. I thought I'd be happy... but now I'm divorced, and....." Ayzen raised a hand, stopping her. "Mahnoor, you don't get to walk back into my life just because things went wrong for you. Whatever we had... it's over." Before Mahnoor could reply, the door opened quietly. Hina stepped in, a bright smile on her face and a lunch box in her hands, but the smile froze the moment she saw them together. Mahnoor turned slightly, her elegant earrings catching the light. For a moment, the room went still.

"I... I didn't know you were busy," Hina said softly, her voice trembling just enough to betray her heart. "I just brought you lunch." She placed the box on his desk, her fingers lingering for a second before she stepped back. "Sorry for interrupting." Her throat tightened as she forced a polite smile, then turned around and left before either of them could stop her. Ayzen took a step forward as if to call her back, but Mahnoor's voice broke the silence again.

"She's... your wife?"

"Yes," Ayzen said sharply, his tone leaving no room for doubt. But his heart was no longer in the room. It had followed Hina out the door. Hina's hands trembled as she walked down the hallway, clutching her dupatta. No... no... no... this can't be true, 'she thought, covering her mouth to stop a sob from escaping. Her heart pounded so hard it hurt.

By the time she reached home, she was shaking. She ran straight to her mother's room and fell into her lap. "Ammi..." her voice broke as tears streamed down her cheeks. "Maybe... maybe I dreamed too much." Her mother stroked her hair gently, trying to calm her, but Hina couldn't stop crying. After what felt like hours, she retreated to her room, closed the door, and lay on the bed. Exhausted, her tears finally lulled her into a restless sleep. Back at the office, Ayzen could barely focus on anything. Mahnoor's presence suddenly felt suffocating. Without a word, he stood up and left the office, ignoring Mahnoor. When he reached home, the house was silent. No laughter, no soft footsteps.

"Hina?" he called, checking every room. Panic began to rise in his chest. He dialled her number; no answer. His hands shook slightly as he called her 'mother'. "Hina is here with me," her mother said softly on the other end. Relief washed over him, but guilt followed right after. He sat down on the couch, his head in his hands.

What must she be feeling right now?

Ayzen couldn't sit still. He grabbed his keys and rushed to the car. The drive felt endless. Every red light burnt through his patience; every turn felt too slow. His hands gripped the steering wheel tighter than ever. His mind kept replaying Hina's face when she had seen Mahnoor, the shock, the pain, and each time it felt like a knife twisting in his chest. When he finally reached Hina's mother's house, he didn't even bother parking properly. He jumped out of the car and rang the bell.

'Some storms are meant to test the heart.'

Hina's mother opened the door with a calm expression, but there was a hint of worry in her eyes. "She's upstairs," she said softly, stepping aside. "She hasn't spoken since she came." Ayzen nodded silently, taking off his shoes before walking in. The house felt heavier than usual, as if it had absorbed Hina's pain. Each step up the staircase echoed in the quiet air. When he reached Hina's room, his heart sank. She was sitting on the floor by her bed, her head buried in her knees, arms hugging herself as if she could hold her breaking heart together. Her hair was loose and messy, her face pale, and her cheeks streaked with dried tears.

"Hina..." His voice was barely a whisper. She looked up, her eyes swollen and red. For a few moments, she just stared at him, her lips trembling, and then turned her face away, unable to bear his presence. "You should go," she said quietly, her voice breaking. "No." He stepped closer and knelt down in front of her, gently reaching for her hand. "Please... look at me." She shook her head, her tears threatening to fall again. "Why was she there, Ayzen?"

Her voice was barely audible, but it was loaded with pain. "Why was Mahnoor in your office?" Ayzen took a deep breath, his chest tightening. "Because she called me. She asked to meet at a café, but I said no. I cut the call. She came to the office anyway."

Ayzen reached out and wiped the tear that slipped down her cheek. "Hina, I need you to trust me. You are my present, my future, not her. I didn't want to hurt you, and I didn't want to see her either. Please believe me."

But Hina couldn't answer. Her heart was too heavy, her thoughts too loud. Without a word, she stood up and walked to the window, staring outside as more tears slid down silently. Ayzen stayed there, kneeling, watching her silently. His chest ached; he wanted to hold her, to take away the pain, but he also knew she needed space. After a long pause, he finally said, "I'll wait for you, Hina. No matter how long it takes." Then he stood and gently caressed Hina's head before quietly leaving the room.

A few minutes after Ayzen left, the room remained silent except for Hina's uneven breathing. She stood by the window, staring at nothing, tears still running down her face. The door creaked softly, and her mother stepped in, her gentle presence filling the space. Without a word, she walked over and sat on the bed, patting the spot beside her. Hina turned slowly, her face tired, her heart exhausted, and then she broke. She collapsed into her mother's lap, clutching her like a child, sobbing until her whole body shook. Her mother stroked her hair, letting her cry as long as she needed. When the sobs softened, she finally spoke. "Beta, listen to me," she said softly.

"Every marriage has storms. Sometimes, they come early. Sometimes, they come later. But running away from them doesn't stop the storm; it just leaves you drenched and alone." Hina sniffled, her fingers clutching the edge of her mother's dress.

"But, Ammi," she whispered, her voice breaking, I thought he would never hurt me."

Her mother tilted her face gently, wiping her tears with the edge of her dupatta. "My daughter, pain does not always mean betrayal. Sometimes it just means life is testing how strong your love really is. You know Ayzen's heart. You know the man he is. Don't let doubts steal your peace." Hina sat up slowly, her breathing still uneven but her mind quieter. Her mother smiled softly and cupped her face. "You love him, don't you?" Hina nodded, a tear slipping down her cheek. "Then go back to him. Don't punish your heart by staying away. Talk to him when you are calm. Tell him how you feel. And remember, Hina, trust is the rope that keeps a marriage standing; don't let it break." Hina took a deep breath, feeling a strange sense of strength slowly return to her chest. That night, she stayed at her mother's house.

The next morning, Hina stood in front of the mirror, fastening her dupatta when a sudden wave of weakness washed over her. Her knees felt shaky, and a strange, sharp pain shot through her bones, leaving her momentarily breathless. She grabbed the edge of the table for support, her reflection blurring as she blinked rapidly. Her hands were colder than usual, her lips pale. For a second, she felt dizzy, almost lightheaded, and there was a dull ache in her back and joints, the kind she had been ignoring for days. But Hina shook her head quickly, refusing to let fear take over.

'Not now. I can't break now.' She thought.

Her heart was set on one thing: going back. Whatever was happening to her body, whatever this sudden pain meant, she could deal with it later. Right now, she needed to face Ayzen. She pressed her dupatta to her chest, whispering a short prayer, hugged her mother tightly, and walked out of the house, her steps slower than usual but filled with determination. Each step toward Ayzen's home felt heavy.

Yet her heart beat faster with every passing minute. When Hina stepped into the house, the air felt thick with silence. She could hear her own heartbeat as she placed her sandals near the door. Ayzen was in the living room, sitting on the edge of the couch, elbows on his knees, his face buried in his hands. The moment he heard her footsteps, he stood up quickly. His normally calm, controlled expression was gone; his eyes were restless, like he hadn't slept all night. "Hina...I knew you would come back" His voice was soft, almost careful, as though one wrong word might shatter her again. She didn't look at him right away. She kept her gaze on the floor as she set her bag down. Her chest felt heavy, her fingers trembling slightly from the weakness still lingering in her body, but she stood tall. "I didn't come back because everything is okay," she said finally, her voice low but steady. "I came back because I can't stay angry at you forever, Ayzen. You are my home." Her words hit him like a storm. In two steps, he was in front of her. He gently lifted her chin, forcing her to meet his eyes.

"I thought I'd lost you," he admitted, his voice raw. "When you walked out yesterday... I've never been that scared in my life. Hina, I swear to you Mahnoor is my past. She means nothing to me. You... you are everything." Hina's throat tightened, tears welling up again.

"Then why does it hurt so much?" she whispered. "Why do I feel like I'm not enough?" Ayzen's chest ached at her words. He cupped her face with both hands, his thumb brushing away her tears.

"You are more than enough," he said firmly. "You are my peace, Hina. My strength. Don't let one moment of doubt take away what we have." Hina's breath shook as she looked into his eyes, and for the first time since yesterday, she saw nothing but truth there. Slowly, almost hesitantly, she rested her forehead against his chest.

His arms wrapped around her tightly, holding her as if he'd never let go. When she finally stepped back, Hina managed a faint smile through her tears. "I want to try again," she said softly. "You don't have to try," Ayzen replied, brushing a strand of hair from her face. "You just have to stay." But as he looked at her closely, his smile faded. There was something about her face, too pale, too tired. Her lips had lost their usual colour, and her shoulders looked frail under the weight of her shawl.

"Hina..." he said carefully, tilting her chin up to meet his eyes. "Are you feeling okay? You look... weak."

Hina quickly shook her head, forcing a small smile. "I'm fine, just tired," she whispered, not wanting to spoil the fragile peace between them. But Ayzen didn't seem convinced. His thumb brushed across her cheek, feeling the slight warmth of her skin. A flicker of worry passed through his eyes. "Promise me you'll tell me if something's wrong," he said quietly. She nodded, even though her heart was pounding. The heaviness in her bones, the strange ache that wouldn't go away. She had felt it again today. But right now, all she wanted was this moment, this closeness, and this safety.

Ayzen pulled her into another hug, holding her as though he could shield her from the entire world. And though Hina closed her eyes, relief washing over her, a small voice in the back of her mind whispered that something was coming, something she could no longer ignore for long.

The next morning, sunlight spilt softly across the curtains, filling the room with a golden glow. Hina woke before the alarm, her body heavy with exhaustion. A dull ache throbbed deep inside her bones, spreading slowly to her arms and legs. She pressed a hand to her chest, feeling her heart beat strangely fast. Her lips felt dry, and there was a faint metallic taste in her mouth. She sat up slowly, gripping the edge of the bed until the dizziness passed.

It's just weakness, she told herself. I'll be fine once I get moving.

The sound of water running from the bathroom snapped her out of her thoughts. Ayzen was getting ready for work. Hina stood, straightened her dupatta, and went to the mirror, forcing a small smile onto her face. Whatever she was feeling inside, she didn't want him to notice.

Minutes later, Ayzen came out, adjusting his cufflinks, looking as effortlessly sharp as always. His tie hung loose around his neck, and Hina stepped forward instinctively, taking it from him. "Here," she said softly, tying the knot with practised hands. Ayzen watched her closely, noticing the way her fingers trembled slightly. "You're quiet this morning," he said, his voice gentle. "I'm just sleepy," she replied,

Avoiding his eyes and finishing the knot neatly. He didn't look convinced, but he didn't press further. Instead, he reached out and tucked a strand of hair behind her ear. "Take it easy today, hmm? Don't tire yourself out." Hina smiled faintly and nodded. She followed him downstairs, watching as he picked up his laptop bag and keys. As always, she walked with him to the front door. When they stepped outside, the morning breeze ruffled her hair. Ayzen turned back to look at her before getting into the car. "Take care," he said warmly. "I will," she whispered, her smile soft but her heart heavy.

He leaned forward and kissed her forehead, a simple gesture that made her chest ache even more. Then he got into the car, started the engine, and drove away. Hina stood there until his car disappeared down the street. Only then did her smile fade. The pain in her legs had returned, sharper now, almost burning. She felt lightheaded again and had to hold the doorframe for support. By the time she went back inside, her mind was made up. She couldn't ignore this any longer. She quickly changed into a simple outfit, tied her hair back, and grabbed her bag. Without telling anyone, she booked a cab and headed to the doctor's clinic, her heart pounding with a mix of fear and determination.

As the cab moved through the streets, she stared out the window, her thoughts racing.

Whatever this is, I need to know. I can't let Ayzen find out like this. Not until I'm sure.

When she finally reached the clinic, her hands were cold. She walked in slowly, her steps heavy, and gave her name at the reception. Then she sat down in the waiting area, her fingers gripping the edge of her shawl. For the first time, Hina prayed not just for her love but for her life.

The waiting room smelt faintly of antiseptic and a hint of jasmine from a nearby vase. She sat on a hard chair, hands clasped tightly in her lap, feeling the tremor in her fingers. Every passing second made the fear in her chest grow heavier. A nurse called her name, and she followed quietly into an examination room. The doctor, a middle-aged woman with kind but serious eyes, motioned her onto the bed. She asked her a series of questions about her fatigue, unexplained bruises, fever, night sweats, and persistent bone pain. Hina answered as honestly as she could, though her voice trembled.

"Let's run some blood tests first," she said gently. A few minutes later, a nurse came in to draw her blood. Hina watched the syringe fill, her stomach twisting with unease. She felt faint and dizzy, gripping the edge of the bed tightly, her breath shallow. Once the blood samples were sent for testing, the doctor asked her to wait. The minutes crawled, and Hina could feel her heart hammering. When the results came back, the doctor studied them carefully, his brows knitting together.

"Hina... I'm afraid the results confirm our suspicions," she said softly, placing a steady hand on her shoulder. "Your white blood cell count is abnormally high, your red blood cells and platelets are low, and the bone marrow shows abnormal blast cells. This indicates 'acute leukaemia'. You need urgent treatment and close monitoring." Hina's stomach lurched. The words seemed to hang in the air, weighty and cruel. "... acute leukaemia?" she whispered, barely able to form the words. She could feel her hands shaking violently now, clutching the edges of the examination bed as if holding on could keep the world from tilting. The doctor nodded solemnly. "I know it's hard to hear, Hina.

We will start treatment as soon as possible. But you must bring your husband next time. He needs to understand everything so he can support you fully."

Hina rose from the bed, legs unsteady, and stepped out into the sunlight. The warmth felt unreal against the cold panic that had settled in her chest. Her thoughts raced, spiralling into a nightmare she couldn't escape.

What if Ayzen... what if he forgets me? What if he moves on with Mahnoor if I... if I die?

Her throat tightened, and tears blurred her vision. Every step toward home felt heavier than the last, as though the world itself was pressing down on her fragile body and fragile heart. By the time she reached the familiar streets of her neighbourhood, her mind was numb with fear, and her tears flowed freely.

Chapter 11

The next morning, Hina waited until Ayzen had finished breakfast and was preparing to leave for work. Her hands trembled slightly as she held a small folder close to her chest. She knew she couldn't hide the truth any longer. "Ayzen... I need to show you something," she said softly, her voice quivering. Ayzen turned, sensing the seriousness in her tone. "What is it, Hina?" he asked, concern knitting his brows. She opened the folder and handed him the neatly organised medical reports, blood tests, and the doctor's notes. "The doctor... says I have acute leukaemia. My condition is critical," she whispered, her eyes searching his for understanding. Ayzen's hand shook as he took the papers, scanning each page. The numbers, the terms, and the doctor's stamp all confirmed her words. He felt the room spin slightly, his chest tightening. "Hina... this... this can't be real," he murmured, his voice thick with disbelief, as tears started welling in his eyes. Hina reached out, placing her hand over his. "It is, Ayzen. I wanted you to know the truth so we can face it together," she said, her voice steady despite the fear in her heart. For a long moment, Ayzen was silent, reading and rereading the reports, letting the reality sink in. Then he finally looked up at her, tears streaking his cheeks, his lips trembling.

"Hina...I can't believe this... No matter what it takes, we will walk on this together," he said firmly, pulling her into his arms. His heartbeat thumped against hers.

Hina clung to him, letting herself feel both the fear and the love. Ayzen wiped her tears, his own hands shaking. "We'll fight this, Hina. Every test, every treatment- you won't face it alone. I swear it," he whispered. From that day, Ayzen became her constant support. He accompanied her for every check-up, carried her medications, and held her hand through every injection. The first days were terrifying, each visit a mix of hope and dread, but Ayzen's presence made it bearable. Slowly, Ayzen's family noticed her struggle and, seeing his unwavering devotion, began to offer her care too. Warm meals, gentle words, and small gestures of kindness wrapped around her like a comforting blanket. Hina's mother also joined in, staying by her side during the hardest moments, brushing her hair, holding her hands, and whispering prayers for strength. In this cocoon of love, Hina began to feel courage she hadn't known before. Even in the shadow of her illness, she felt she could breathe; she could fight, because Ayzen's hand was always there to hold hers.

The morning air was crisp as Ayzen helped Hina into the car, her scarf loosely draped over her shoulders. Even on bad days, he made sure she felt safe, secure, and loved. "Ready, Hina?" he asked gently, buckling her seatbelt. She nodded, gripping the edge of her seat, her heart a mix of hope and fear.

Another check-up... another day of treatments... But I'll survive. I have to...

As they drove through the quiet streets, Hina leaned back, closing her eyes, letting the sunlight warm her face. For a moment, she felt a fragile peace. But that calm shattered when Ayzen slowed the car near the hospital entrance, and a familiar figure appeared across the driveway. Mahnoor dressed impeccably, her hair shining under the sun, a confident smile playing on her lips.

Hina's eyes widened, an icy wave of fear and jealousy crawling up her spine. Ayzen's grip on her hand didn't waver, and he didn't even glance at Mahnoor as she approached, waving politely. He opened the car door and helped Hina out, positioning himself slightly between them.

"Good morning," Mahnoor said softly, tilting her head. Ayzen's eyes didn't meet hers. "Good Morning," he replied curtly, guiding Hina toward the hospital entrance. Every step was deliberate, protective, and unyielding. As the elevator carried them up to the oncology floor, Hina's hands trembled. Silent tears rolled down her cheeks.

What if I die someday? She thought, her chest tightening. What if she... gets close to him? She pressed her hands to her face, trying to stop the tears.

No... he is mine... only mine...

Mahnoor lingered near the hospital entrance long after Ayzen and Hina disappeared into the treatment room. Her sharp eyes had caught a glimpse of the medical reports as Ayzen carried the folder, and a cruel satisfaction twisted in her chest. So, she's sick... seriously sick, she thought, and her lips curled into a small, cold smile.

Maybe now... Maybe now he will be mine again.

She imagined herself stepping into Hina's place, the devoted wife who needed protection, the woman Ayzen would lean on. Every scenario played out vividly in her mind:

Him holding her hand, comforting her, trusting her, loving her. The idea sent a shiver of excitement through her.

He will need me... and I'll be there... He's mine again.

Mahnoor didn't consider the pain of seeing Hina, suffer or the quiet bravery Hina displayed as she fought fear and illness. She only saw opportunity. Her fingers tightened around her purse strap as she plotted silently, already envisioning herself taking advantage of this fragile moment in Hina's life. Inside, Hina sat in the treatment room, unaware of Mahnoor's scheming. Every injection, every test, every sharp ache in her bones made her heart ache, but what hurt even more was the thought of Ayzen possibly being dragged into Mahnoor's web. She glanced at Ayzen clenching his hand as tears welled up.

Meanwhile, Mahnoor's smile widened outside, eyes glinting with malicious intent. For the first time in months, she felt hope, a twisted, selfish hope that life's cruel hand had dealt her a chance to reclaim what she thought was hers. And she intended to make sure she took it.

A few days later, Ayzen was seated at his office desk, papers neatly stacked, phone buzzing intermittently. He was still thinking about Hina, her fragile state, and the exhaustion that showed in her eyes the previous day. His mind was focused on work, but every few minutes, he caught himself glancing at the clock, wishing he could be with her instead. Then the office door swung open, and Mahnoor appeared, her heels clicking against the polished floor. She looked impeccable, her hair perfectly styled, a confident smile painted across her face. But her eyes were sharp, calculating. Ayzen froze, a cold pulse running through him, and instinctively straightened in his chair.

"H-hello, Ayzen," she said smoothly, as if her sudden appearance was completely normal. "Mahnoor," he said, keeping his voice firm. "What are you doing here?" She leaned lightly against the edge of his desk, tilting her head. "I thought... we could talk. Like old times." Her gaze flickered toward the phone on his desk, imagining the chance to rekindle what she had lost. Ayzen didn't flinch. He picked up a file and began flipping through it, deliberately avoiding her gaze. "I'm busy. I don't have time," he said, keeping his tone polite but distant. Inside, he bristled, anger and irritation boiling quietly. Not now. Not ever. Hina is my wife.

Mahnoor's eyes narrowed slightly, sensing the barrier he had built. She tried to lean closer, but before she could speak again, Ayzen's assistant knocked lightly on the door and announced lunch delivery. He took that moment and left the office for lunch. While Mahnoor stands there thinking

How could he...? She thought, her hands curling into fists at her sides. He once loved me so completely. Every glance, every word... And now... He won't even look at me.

Her jealousy twisted into something sharper, darker. She felt an urge to interfere, to reclaim a hold she once had over him, but deep down she knew Hina wasn't just any woman. And no matter how badly Mahnoor wanted it, she couldn't break what had formed between Ayzen and Hina. Mahnoor stood there, burning with memories of a love that once defined him and realising, with a sinking heart, that it no longer had a place in his present. Ayzen was halfway through his lunch when his phone rang. The name flashing on the screen made his heart skip a beat; it was his sister, Aleeza. "Ayzen... you need to come, quickly," her voice trembled with urgency. "Hina... she's fainted at home. They're rushing her to the hospital." The world seemed to narrow around him. Fork still in hand, he jumped up, heart pounding so hard he thought it would burst. "I'm coming," he gasped, abandoning everything. He raced out, the car engine roaring beneath him, each red light and slow turn torturing him with the thought of his wife in danger.

When he finally reached the hospital, he sprinted inside, ignoring the receptionist and following Aleeza's panicked instructions to the ICU. There she was, his love, pale and dull, her breathing shallow, and hands trembling weakly. His chest tightened, and he stumbled to her side, taking her hand in his, feeling how fragile she had become. "Hina... meri jaan... Look at me," he whispered, tears welling up in his eyes. She opened her eyes slightly, a faint flicker of recognition, and she smiled. She squeezed his hand weakly, clutching him as if he were the only anchor left in the world. "Promise me, Ayzen..." she whispered, her voice barely audible but dripping with love. "I... I have loved you... more than words can ever say." Her thumb brushed across his cheek, tracing the edge of his jaw like she wanted to keep every detail of him with her.

"Don't cry for me, my love... Promise me you will stay strong... even if I'm not here... please..." Her voice trembled with effort, and she gasped slightly, trying to keep the words flowing. "Be happy... for both of us... Live your life with a smile... And don't forget... I will always be with you...In your heart, in your memories... everywhere." Ayzen shook his head violently, tears streaming freely down his face.

"No... love... Don't say that... I can't... I can't live without you..." Hina's hand lingered on his face, pressing gently, as if she wanted to imprint herself onto him forever. "Shh... listen to me... I want... you to be strong... always. And... I will wait... for you... in a place where we can... meet again."

Her hands began to loosen from his shirt. He felt the warmth leave her grip, felt her life slip away like sand through his fingers. Reality crashed down on him with a force he couldn't bear. His Hina... his world... was gone. He screamed her name, his voice cracking with unbearable pain. "Meri jaan! Meri jaan!" His tears fell in torrents, drenching her frail hands as he clutched her lifeless form, refusing to let go. The world blurred around him

Chapter 12

They reached home with a heavy heart. Ayzen moved through the house like a shadow, his heart heavy and his eyes hollow. Every corner reminded him of Hina, her laughter, the way she arranged the cushions, the soft hum she would make while folding laundry, and the gentle way she had always cared for everyone around her. Each memory cut through him like a knife. Preparations for Hina's final rites began, and the reality of her absence hit everyone like a storm. Ayzen's family, who had never fully appreciated her warmth and patience, now sat in stunned silence, with tears quietly falling. They whispered her name, remembering how calm and kind she had been despite all the small cruelties they had shown her. Guilt weighed heavily on their hearts.

Hina's mother could not stop crying. She had only Hina, her daughter, her heart, her world, and now she was gone. Each sob shook her small frame, her hands clutching the empty space where Hina's warmth had been. She whispered apologies and regrets aloud, wishing she could have done more, held her tighter, and told her she was loved every single day. Zara and Aleeza, who had shared laughter, secrets, and dreams with Hina, felt a hollow ache deep inside. They missed their friend more than words could say. The thought that they would never hear her voice again, never see her smile, and never share a simple moment of joy, broke them.

Their hearts ached with the unfairness of life that someone so kind and beautiful could be taken away so soon. Even Anoosha, who had once watched Hina with jealousy and resentment, now sat in silence, staring at the floor. The feelings of hatred, the games she had played, and the whispers she had spread-all of it now felt meaningless, shallow, and cruel. She had lost the chance to know a heart like Hina's, to be her friend instead of her rival. Her eyes filled with tears as she whispered to herself,

Life is short just like this... Why did I waste it with jealousy, hatred, and betrayal? Why couldn't I have been kind?

The guilt gnawed at her soul, and she vowed silently never to let envy control her again. The funeral was quiet and solemn. Each person there held a piece of Hina's memory in their hearts. As the ceremony ended, everyone lingered, unable to leave completely, feeling the weight of her absence. The air was thick with grief, yet there was also a silent lesson in the loss: the importance of cherishing the people we love, the fleeting moments we take for granted, and the words left unsaid. Hina had given so much of herself quietly, never asking for recognition, and now that she was gone, her impact was clear: love, kindness, and patience could leave a mark stronger than anything else. And somewhere deep in their hearts, those who had known her friends, family, even those who had once envied her- learnt the most valuable truth:

Cherish every moment with the people you love, forgive, show kindness, and never let bitterness or jealousy cloud your heart. Life is fleeting, and sometimes, it is only when someone is gone that we realise how precious love, trust, and care truly are. Hina's absence left a hollow, aching space, yet her presence lingered in memories, in lessons, and in hearts that had loved her.

And that, in the end, was the gift she had left behind: the reminder that a pure soul, even gone too soon, can forever change the world of those who loved her.

Months passed.......

Since Hina's departure her presence was felt in every corner of home. The walls still carried her gentle touch, the small decorations she had arranged, and the soft hum of memories that played like a song in Ayzen's heart. Ayzen had changed. His grief was deep, but it had transformed into a quiet strength. Every morning, he would sit by the window, holding a cup of tea, and whisper small words of love to Hina as if she were still there. He had taken her lessons to heart- patience, kindness, and unconditional love- and carried them into his life, not just for himself, but for the people around him. Hina's mother found solace in knowing that her daughter's memory lived on in Ayzen. She often visited, bringing warmth, laughter, and stories of Hina's life. Even in her sorrow, she smiled softly, proud of how Hina had left an indelible mark on everyone she had loved.

Even Anoosha had changed. She carried the weight of her past jealousy and betrayal as a reminder of how cruel envy could be. She became gentler, more aware, and determined never to let bitterness rule her heart again. Hina had unknowingly left a legacy, teaching everyone that life is too short for hate, and love should always guide us.

Ayzen, standing in the quiet of the evening, looked out at the horizon, feeling the gentle wind brush against his face. He whispered,

"Hina... my beautiful wife... You will always be with me." And in that moment, he felt her presence soft and warm, reminding him that love, once true and pure, never fades. Life moved on, but Hina's memory remained eternal. Her laughter, her patience, and her kindness all lived on in the hearts of those she had touched. And in their lives, she became more than a memory; she became a guiding light, teaching them the power of love, the importance of cherishing every moment, and the beauty of a soul who had loved without measure.

'We cannot hold on to what time takes, but memories can Make even loss beautiful.'

• • • •

Dear Readers,

IF YOU EVER FEEL JEALOUSY or anger toward someone, remember Hina's story. Life is too short to waste on hatred or grudges. Every moment with the people you care about is precious, and you never know how long you will have them. Be kind, be patient, and show love every day, because even small acts of care can mean the world to someone. Don't wait to say sorry, don't wait to forgive, and don't wait to tell someone how much they matter. Embrace every smile, every shared moment, because once it is gone, you cannot bring it back. Love fully, forgive freely, and hold the people you care about close, for **tomorrow is never promised.**

• • • •

THOUGH THIS ENDS, SOME hearts will always remember it.

@HIMA_SARFAS

Every story leaves a mark, and so does every reader. Write down what this book made you feel and send a picture of it to my email [fhimana.official@gmail.com] or by scanning the QR code to reach me on Instagram. Your words will mean the world to me, and with your permission, I may share some of them with other readers. Thank you for being part of this journey.

About the Author

Fathima Himana, born in Kandy, Sri Lanka, is a passionate storyteller who believes that every heart carries an untold story. Suno Kahani Meri is her debut novel, written straight from the soul, weaving emotions and experiences into words that speak to readers. With a deep love for literature and creativity, she aspires to inspire others to listen to their own stories within.

www.ingramcontent.com/pod-product-compliance
Lightning Source LLC
LaVergne TN
LVHW090418210926
848480LV00002B/609